⟨ W9-AVR-678

Getting Lucky

A FORTUNE, COLORADO NOVEL

JENNIFER SEASONS

AVONIMPULSE

An Imprint of HarperCollinsPublishers

To Amye,
Because of your spirit, your strength, and your heart.
I love you, lady.

This is a work of fiction. Names, characters, places, and incidents are products of the author's imagination or are used fictitiously and are not to be construed as real. Any resemblance to actual events, locales, organizations, or persons, living or dead, is entirely coincidental.

Excerpt from *Talking Dirty* copyright © 2015 by Candice Wakoff.

GETTING LUCKY. Copyright © 2015 by Candice Wakoff. All rights reserved under International and Pan-American Copyright Conventions. By payment of the required fees, you have been granted the nonexclusive, nontransferable right to access and read the text of this e-book on screen. No part of this text may be reproduced, transmitted, decompiled, reverse-engineered, or stored in or introduced into any information storage and retrieval system, in any form or by any means, whether electronic or mechanical, now known or hereafter invented, without the express written permission of HarperCollins e-books.

EPub Edition APRIL 2015 ISBN: 9780062365033

Print Edition ISBN: 9780062365026

AM 10 9 8 7 6 5 4 3 2 1

Chapter One

"BE PREPARED TO use the ladies." Her sister pointed at her chest.

Shannon Charlemagne released a groan and bit her tongue, her patience already on the verge of deserting her. Her sister's rather unhelpful suggestion about her breasts at this particular moment had that patience packing its bags and furiously scribbling a Dear John letter on a sticky note.

The crap her family put her through.

Pushing away from the hood of the rental car she'd been sitting on, Shannon glanced at the entrance to a horse ranch in the mountains outside Fortune, Colorado, and sighed heavily. Where would she be without her patience? It was her armor, her protection. Losing it would be worse than being thrown to a bunch of wild jackals with bacon-wrapped sausages strung around her head like a Christmas wreath. And with the insanity she was about to fling herself into, she needed it more than ever. Not for the first time, she wondered how she'd been roped into such a stupid situation.

Oh, that's right, because she could never really put her foot down and say no when it mattered.

If she had a dime for every time her family obligated her to something against her will, she'd be richer than Oprah and living it up on Martinique with a French cabana boy named Pierre.

Sometimes she really wished she were part of a nice, average, *normal* family. One where there weren't so many expectations to live up to the legacy that was her family birthright. So much pressure to conform. She was a Charlemagne—the oldest and most prestigious family in all of American horseracing. The most renowned and well-respected family in the industry.

Yeah, it was like that. She was one of *those* Charlemagnes.

Which ultimately meant that, as much as she balked (which wasn't as much as she'd prefer, granted), deep down she was a good girl who was loyal to a fault and never went against her father. No matter how overbearing and authoritative he might be. She understood her duties and responsibilities to the Charlemagne name.

Didn't mean she had to like it, though.

Sighing again, Shannon pushed back a clump of her light auburn hair that had fallen loose from the braid she'd hastily made that morning and resigned herself to her ill-conceived fate. Her father had asked her to do this. Good idea or bad, it didn't matter. He'd said it was important for the family—crucial even.

And that's why, even though she disagreed with pretty much every aspect of his request, she was currently standing on a gravel road in the Colorado mountains about to do something not entirely on the up-and-up. She and her sister were squinting against the brilliant afternoon sun as they gave the plan one last run-through before she set off alone into the great unknown.

Still, there *were* limits to what she was willing to do, family or not.

"Why does everything always have to be about sex with you?" Shannon asked. She pointed a finger at her breasts, giving her sister a slight frown. "You know these ladies only come out for very special occasions. They're highly selective. And this, shall we say, *undercover* job I'm about to partake in, certainly doesn't qualify."

"Does too," Colleen scoffed. "Your boobs come out far too infrequently, if you ask my opinion," her sister added, somehow managing simultaneously to sound both affronted and amused. Colleen didn't usually wait for anyone to ask her thoughts. She just spoke her mind. Whether or not her opinion was wanted was, often, a toss-up.

"And why would I do that?"

"Because I'm practically a doctor? As an upcoming graduate of Harvard Medical School, it's my almost-professional opinion that you don't have nearly enough sex."

Shannon laughed outright at that. There her little sister went saying crazy things again. "Thank you so much for caring about my love life and well-being, but I think I'll be fine."

Humor shimmered in her sister's hazel eyes as she tipped her head toward the huge Pine Creek Ranch sign that hung suspended from wooden beams arching over the entrance. Her blond hair brushed across her freckled cheeks as she said, "I wouldn't be so hasty in keeping those girls on the shelf if I were you...I saw Sean Muldoon in person."

"When?"

"During the races in Kentucky this past May with his Triple Crown winner, Something Unexpected. This guy that Dad is sending you to spy on is full-on Irish—with the accent to prove it—and downright sexy. He's like an Irish Dove bar—you know just by looking at him that he's dark, smooth, and addictive. He moves with this loose, long-limbed gate and has an easy smile, but there's something almost dangerous about him just bubbling under the surface. It's seriously potent." Colleen fanned herself and grinned. "It's too bad I'm such a blabber-mouth, because I'd dig up the goods on him, all right."

Shannon remained silent and waited for it. It had to be coming.

"Of course, I'd see if Muldoon was as fast to the finish line as his racehorses are while I was at it, if you know what I mean." Her sister finished with an overly dramatic eyebrow wiggle and wink.

And there it was. Right on schedule. That's one of the things she loved most about her only sibling—she was reliable. If there was ever an opening for a crude comment to be slipped in, you could bet she was all over it.

That's what she said, Shannon thought.

Crap! Damn it, now Colleen had her doing it too. Figured.

"Let's go through this one last time," Shannon said briskly. "I'm supposed to find this Sean Muldoon and tell him I'm responding to his ad for the stable manager position and convince him to hire me." She stared down the long gravel lane beyond the ranch's entrance as it lazily rounded a bend and disappeared into a sea of aspen, spruce, and pine in the distance.

Into Sean Muldoon's ranch.

She'd learned from her father that Pine Creek sat on about one hundred acres, though it was hard to tell at the moment from the thick grove of trees that flanked each side of the single-lane road. It looked more like the entrance to a state forest, not a sprawling horse ranch.

But, as Shannon knew better than most, looks were most often deceiving. Nervously swiping her hands down the thighs of her worn denim jeans, she continued reviewing the plan that their father had designed, hoping that repeating everything would help her focus.

Colleen opened her mouth and started to say, "That's why you should—"

Shannon held her hand up like a crossing guard. "I know, use the ladies. I get it." She probably could if she wanted to, honestly. They weren't bad. A quick glance downward confirmed that claim. Not bad at all. A little on the small side, but so what? What she lacked up top she made up for on the bottom with an ample and curvy derriere.

Depending on the day, that was either a blessing or a curse.

However, given that she was a professional equestrian and spent half her life bouncing around on a horse (with skill and grace, of course), having the extra padding was more often a bonus than not. Her butt was like a car's suspension system—it absorbed the shock and made the impact of jumping her horse feel like the smooth ride of a Rolls Royce. Not that she was going to upstage big-butted celebrities or anything, but it wouldn't be a runaway victory if they *did* compare backsides. Only she had earned hers the cheap and easy way: genetic inheritance.

Colleen cleared her throat. "Dad's gut is saying that either Muldoon or one of his trainers is doping the Thoroughbreds with steroids before the races." Her sister's eyes flickered and unfocused briefly, like she was recalling a memory. "I've seen them run. They've got rockets for hooves, Shan."

No wonder all of the company's clients had bailed on their breeding program over the past few years. Shannon knew they were down to a teeny-tiny trickle, and if she didn't find a way to reverse that fast, then they were going to go bankrupt and lose the farm. And it was the only thing of material value they had left. Over the years her father had sold off everything else. All the jewels, cars— everything. It hadn't escaped her notice that the walls of her childhood home were now mostly bare, when priceless Monet originals and the like had once hung there.

Not for the first time, she wondered what had happened to all the family's money. Where were all their millions disappearing to? It didn't make sense. Not in the least. But pondering that made Shannon's stomach go tight and queasy, so she stopped. With effort she grappled with her thoughts and redirected them to the immediate problem at hand.

Shannon glanced at a stand of early June aspens swaying in the gentle breeze and smiled softly. The leaves were such a tender shade of green against the white of the bark; there wasn't anything like them back home in Saratoga Springs, New York, which was too bad because they were beautiful. The leaves danced on the wind like gypsies around a campfire.

"It's beautiful here." She couldn't help admitting it. Even the sunshine on her face felt amazing. "It's such a gorgeous day, isn't it? If this guy doesn't hire me, I'll hike back down to the entrance here and meet you. I'll text you once I know if I got the job."

Colleen shifted and crossed her arms, her voice oddly neutral when she replied, "Of course. I was planning to wait."

Shannon narrowed her eyes, suddenly suspicious of her sister's tone. "Did Dad tell you to leave me here anyway?" It would be so like him to force his will on her even from two thousand miles away. No way did she want to be stranded out in the wilds of the Colorado Rockies with no transportation. It was something like seven miles back into town. Not exactly a leisurely afternoon stroll in the park.

"I'm sorry, Shan, but I have to. You know how Dad is. In his mind, you'll work harder to secure the job if you don't have any backup waiting for you. He called it 'added incentive.'" Sympathy and understanding shone in her eyes. They both knew all too well what that meant. "I wish I could stay here to make sure it all goes well, but I can't. My orders are to head straight back to the hotel and call Dad to receive instructions. Before you ask, I have no idea what he has planned for me."

Instinctively Shannon's back went up. Callum Charlemagne was so very fond of his orders. How else best to rule the kingdom, right?

Feeling that old tension settle between her shoulder blades, Shannon began to pace. Some things just never changed, no matter how old she was. His penchant for bullying made her as angry today as it had when she was a teenager.

Colleen placed a hand on her arm, gently stopping her midstride. "He loves us, Shannon. In his way, the best he can. And he legitimately needs your help." Her fingers gripped tightly for a brief moment and then released, her expression suddenly pensive. "This time we all do."

That simple truth took the fire out of Shannon. They all needed her to step up. Her family was the majority shareholder in the company, but for how much longer, no one knew. They'd had to borrow against the stock, and there was no money to repay the loan since they had so few clients generating cash flow.

No income, no majority control of the company—no farm.

Why? Because her *family* farm was owned by the company. And without the security of owning 51 percent of the stock, they could be booted off the place without a moment's notice. In every way, they and the business—their very *future*—would be at the whim of the company.

It still grated, knowing that truth. Not only had the business been in the Charlemagne line for generations, the farm was home. It held all their best memories—like how every Christmas her mother made homemade cinnamon rolls with cream cheese frosting for breakfast and everyone sat in front of the fireplace with their newly opened gifts and chowed down. They all got to eat with their fingers. It was *heaven*.

And in all actuality, it was the one time of year that her parents really and truly relaxed. They laughed and smiled, and seemed to leave the bad stuff behind—or at least alone. The rest of the year the stress of simply being a Charlemagne and managing everything that entailed wore them down. Christmas was their time to breathe.

It had been tough growing up with parents who were too busy maintaining the family name to spend any quality time with their children, but she'd had Colleen. As much as her sister made her sometimes want to wash her mouth out with soap and sit her down with a wholesome Hallmark made-for-TV movie to cleanse her corrupted brain, she was thankful every single day for her.

It helped telling herself that dissecting cadavers during medical school had warped her lovely sister's mind, so having it permanently in the gutter wasn't her fault.

She was joking.

Mostly.

Taking a big breath to help soothe her quivering stomach, she gave her sister's hand a quick squeeze. "You're right. I know you are. I just get so frustrated with him sometimes, you know?"

Colleen pulled her in for a swift all-business hug, the time for emotion clearly behind them. "I know. But hey, think of this adventure as fodder you can use later to write that Great American Novel you've always dreamed about."

A snort escaped Shannon. "Clearly you're delusional if you think I want to write a novel, much less have the capability," she couldn't help teasing.

Colleen rolled her eyes and gave Shannon's arm a playful shove. "See what I get for being sympathetic? Sarcasm. I get sarcasm and derision from my only and most beloved sibling." Her expression remained serious for a moment, but Shannon knew it was about to crack. Seconds later a grin split her deceptively wholesome face and she laughed. "Thank God I'm rarely sympathetic, or else that might hurt."

Shannon laughed at that. Sensitivity wasn't the youngest Charlemagne's strong suit. Not by a long shot. It was one of the things that made her so incredibly strong. And it was one of the main reasons she was at the top of her class at Harvard. She was the most goal-oriented person Shannon had ever known. Colleen didn't let pesky things like emotions get in the way of her achieving her dreams.

If only she could say the same for herself.

At that moment a very large semitruck rounded the bend in the highway behind them and lumbered past, its trailer swaying from the constant turns along the tight mountain roads. When the flannel-clad driver spotted the two of them on the side of the road, he blared his horn and made a highly inappropriate hand gesture out the window toward them. It seemed that she and her sister were being invited to take a little lap nap with him.

"In your dreams, jerk!" Colleen yelled to the retreating semitruck, making a hand gesture of her own, and then gave Shannon an incredulous look. "Can you believe that guy?" Shannon shrugged and started to talk, but Colleen cut her off by exclaiming, "Like I'd ever do that with a guy who wore *flannel*!"

Her sister sounded so offended that Shannon couldn't stop the burst of laughter that let loose. "Heaven forbid!"

Colleen leveled her with a stare and said flatly, "It was plaid, Shannon. *Plaid.*"

Trying to wrangle her laughter but finding the effort futile, she gave into the giggle fit and braced herself against the rental car for support. It occurred to her the laughter might be misplaced nerves and that she was really just an anxiety-ridden mess over the duplicitous mission she was about embark upon.

But then again, maybe not. The look of horror on her sister's face at the thought of sleeping with a guy who wore plaid flannel was outright hilarious. And priceless. Turns out, there actually *was* one thing in this world that could make the unflappable Colleen Charlemagne flappable.

"What about this Sean Muldoon?" Shannon asked her sister after the giggles had subsided and she could speak again. "You said he's pretty hot. Would you do him if he wore plaid flannel?"

Colleen appeared to contemplate the question, but only made a little hum in her throat. "Dad's waiting,

Shan. Why don't you get this show on the road and find out for yourself?"

Sighing at the twinge of guilt that told her she was indeed procrastinating and they both knew it, Shannon took one more calming breath and then grabbed her small duffle bag from the backseat. Everything she needed was in there. Much as she didn't like the truth, it was time to do this thing.

Suddenly swamped with anxiety, she spun to her sister. "I can do this, right?"

Receiving a fierce hug in response, Shannon squared her shoulders and settled the duffle bag strap more comfortably across her body. She glanced down the long lane again and felt her insides shiver. She could do this. No big thing.

All that was at stake was *everything*.

Chapter Two

IF SEAN MULDOON had to look at one more Excel spreadsheet today, he was going to punch something. Hard. And probably more than once. Technology wasn't his thing. Not by a long shot. Even computers with software designed to help a person crunch numbers into tidy, organized little rows were enough to give him a migraine.

He wasn't made for this shite.

For a guy who'd grown up on the backstreets of Dublin, Ireland—where bare knuckles were the universal language—the enormous increase in computer work was paramount to torture. It hadn't been so bad before his boy Something Unexpected had won the Triple Crown last year. But ever since then, it had increasingly felt like a full-time job.

One that he was no longer feeling stubborn enough to muddle his way through on his own.

Why hadn't he listened to his mates Aidan and Jake last month when they'd encouraged him to hire a stable manager? It had been a dumb-shite move on his part to dismiss the applicants who'd called after the guys had placed an ad for him anyway. With the leap in the ranch's popularity the past year, his once-quiet home was now permeated with the sound of the telephone ringing off the hook. People were begging to be put on the breeding program waiting list and given personal facility tours.

A frustrated sound rumbled in Sean's chest when the numbers on the screen he'd highlighted turned into some alien language of symbols instead of neatly adding up the selected column like he'd been expecting. Scraping his fingers through his shaggy black hair, he scowled at the screen, muttering, "Feck me already."

"Excuse me?"

Sean shoved away from the desk and froze in midchair-rotation, his stomach tightening with the movement. The feminine-sounding voice coming from the doorway had his instincts jumping to alert—and not in the most pleasant of ways. For a brief moment, he shut his eyes and prayed his sudden suspicion was wrong.

People weren't just showing up at his place now too, were they? What, were nonstop phone calls not enough anymore? He was grateful for the business, really he was. But this was too much.

It was even worse than the women who'd hounded him for being one of the so-called Bachelors of Fortune.

Sean felt irritation creep into his chest and took a deep breath. If it was true, and random visitors were in his future, then he needed that stable manager in the worst way. He needed a buffer. There was no way he'd survive another month of fielding telephone calls *and* impromptu visitors, especially since a low profile and privacy were necessities for a guy like Sean. Even though he'd disappeared from the Irish mob scene long ago, pissed-off mob bosses tended not to cap revenge timetables with something as stupid as a statute of limitations.

Forcefully relaxing his muscular shoulders, Sean slowly spun back around as he began with a slight grimace, "Welcome to Pine Creek Ra—"

Suddenly his lungs seemed to deflate right inside his chest and air was hard to come by. There, standing in the doorway of the office, was the warmest, sexiest-looking woman he'd ever seen. She looked like autumn with her long reddish-brown hair and big, rich brown eyes. As she stepped through the doorway, he noticed that her face was covered in a light dusting of freckles, like cinnamon had been sprinkled over the top of her and some had stuck to her skin.

Out of nowhere, he had the strongest urge to know if she smelled like it too. Shaking his head at his odd thoughts, Sean cleared his throat and began again as if his heart wasn't pounding slowly and heavily in his chest, "Welcome to Pine Creek Ranch. Can I help you?"

If she said she was there to lobby for an open schedule spot, then she was in luck. Because looking at her now, he just couldn't seem to find one single reason why he shouldn't give her a spot—or heck, even give her someone else's. Clearly she needed it worse than they did. Why, she'd driven all the way out to his ranch to make the request in person!

All that hemming and hawing he'd been doing about random visitors wasn't serious.

Or was it?

He thought about it for a second. No, it was. It just didn't apply to pretty women who looked like fall and had the most sumptuous hair he'd ever seen. That was fair, right?

Of course it was. He made the rules.

"I'm looking for Sean Muldoon."

Jesus, even her voice was full of warmth. "You found him. I'm Sean."

Because he was busy studying her pretty face, he didn't miss the slight rounding of her eyes at the mention of his name. "You are?" she said.

He couldn't help laughing and replied with a quick, crooked grin. "That's what me mum tells me."

Two little round rose patches colored her cheeks. "I'm sorry. I just didn't expect—I mean, you're so *Irish*. I was anticipating more cowboy."

"Is it the accent?" he teased, even though he knew that was only part of it.

No doubt rightfully, people assumed that since he owned a horse ranch in Colorado, he had to be some Irish version of John Wayne. It often surprised them to discover that he wasn't. Not that he wasn't rugged and masculine and all that shite, but it hadn't come from wrangling horses on a ranch all day.

It had come from bare-knuckle boxing his way up from the back alleys of Dublin, fighting with sweat and

blood to make something of himself. It was that tough-
ness, combined with his penchant for wearing his beloved
Irish wool cap, that threw people off. He'd considered
switching to the typical cowboy hat, but that just hadn't
been right. In fact, he'd felt like a bloody fool the one
time he'd given it a go. One look in the mirror and he'd
decided to just feck it and be himself. To hell with anyone
who had a problem with it. Besides, Irish horsemen didn't
wear ten-gallon hats, cowboy boots, and spurs—yet they
bred some of the best horses around. Was anybody confused by them?

Stereotyping was a funny thing.

His guest smiled at his joke. "I admit, the accent is
stronger than I'd anticipated. But anyway." She strode
across the room toward him and held out a hand, all cordial business. "It's nice to meet you, Sean Muldoon. I'm
Shannon."

Reaching for her outstretched hand, he said, "Ah, an
Irish lass. What can I do for you, Shannon?"

When their hands connected, a jolt shot up his arm
at the soft feminine feel of hers. His work-hardened hand
swallowed her slender one whole.

"I'm here about the stable manager position. Is the
spot still open?"

Surprise jarred him and he automatically shook his
head. "I didn't place that ad; my friends did, even after I
told them not to bother." And it was still a little irritating.
For the past week he'd had those calls to fend off, too.

She tilted her head to the side and frowned slightly.
"Oh, it was a Craigslist ad from the Internet listed just

last week." She began reaching into the back pocket of her jeans. "I've got a copy of it right here."

Sean took the worn and folded piece of paper from her and smoothed it flat. He quickly scanned the contents. "If you'd stopped by last week like another applicant did, I'd have probably sent you on your way, but I'm really fed up with computer work. I don't get it. We're incompatible, me and computers."

As he watched, she smiled and her loose braid slid over her shoulder, the tip settling over her right breast. Her very-nice, very-shapely breast. He pretended not to notice. Mostly.

"I can definitely help you out with that, Mr. Muldoon. Why don't I sit and tell you about my qualifications?"

Before he could utter a word, she'd planted herself in one of the old wooden chairs that abutted the desk, dropping a black bag at her side. "I grew up with horses. I love them and understand them. But, more importantly as I'm seeing, I know computers. If you hire me, not only will I keep the stable itself running smoothly, but all that accounting work and phone calling that's such a pain will all be part of my job—not yours."

Hot damn.

The prospect of never having to deal with accounting software ever again was enough to make him want to hire her on the spot. Well, that and the fact that having *her* around every day to look at wouldn't be much of a hardship. Plus, she could keep the stream of strangers calling off his back. And God forbid if they actually did start showing up on his doorstep.

When he'd first come to the States some five years ago, he'd never expected to find such popularity. Nor had he been looking for it. Exactly the opposite, if truth were told.

He'd wanted to disappear.

But fate was a fickle son of a bitch. Now that he had made a name for himself, there were some very real, very serious concerns about his visibility.

Because good ol' Mickey "Mad Dog" O'Banion might not take kindly to discovering the fact he was still alive.

Giving himself a mental shake, Sean leaned back in his chair and laced his fingers together across his flat stomach, trying for casual. "Where are you from, Shannon?" Her accent was different from the locals of Fortune. To him, everyone else had accents, not him.

As he watched, she crossed legs that were both slender and shapely at the same time, the worn denim snug around them, encasing them in a very tantalizing fashion. He felt his own jeans become a bit tighter across the front as a part of him began to wake.

Sexy women in faded jeans were a total turn on.

"I'm from back East."

"Kentucky?" He didn't know why he was so curious to know where she called home, but he was.

She shook her head and her gorgeous hair shimmered like banked fire in the afternoon sunlight that trickled in through the window behind him. "No, I'm from Saratoga Springs, New York."

His eyebrows shot to his hairline. Saratoga was famous for its racehorses. In fact, one of his biggest competitors lived there. "One of my favorite places," he said pleasantly. "You say you grew up with horses. Is your family in racing then?"

Her gaze held steady on his as she leaned forward in her chair and placed her elbows on her knees. From his new vantage point, he could see directly down the front of her gray V-neck T-shirt. The skin there was milky pale and covered with more of those cinnamon-colored freckles. It took a whole lot of willpower not to openly stare, but he couldn't stop his physical response to the sight of her gorgeous cleavage on display like that.

Belatedly his brain registered that she was speaking and he jerked his gaze back to hers, tuning in to hear her saying, "Of a sort. I spent a lot of time at the Saratoga track, but mostly in the stables with the horses. Yet another reason you should hire me." She finished with a smile meant to be persuasive.

It was. Or rather, she was. *All* of her.

Sean was most definitely feeling persuaded. "You swear you can take that fecking computer off my hands before I throw it out the window?" he said with a nod toward the ancient Mac desktop.

Humor sparked in her big brown eyes and she chuckled. "Bet you're not much of a TV guy either, are you?"

Sean smiled fast and sharp, amused by her comment. It was sarcastic and insightful at the same time. He liked that. "Don't even have one. Do nothing but rot me brain if I sit in front of one long enough."

She laughed and they grinned at each other. "What do you say, Muldoon? How about you hire me and let me save you from the tortures of QuickBooks?"

The lure was there, for sure. Like a Titian siren she beckoned to him, promising deliverance from the drudgery of office work. Her rich brown eyes sucked him in and he was on the verge of saying yes. Maybe he should run a background check, ask for references…

The phone rang, startling them both. Sean leaned forward and began to reach for the receiver when Shannon snatched it from the cradle before he got there. With a wink in his direction, she spoke into the mouthpiece. "Pine Creek Ranch, this is Shannon speaking. How may I help you?"

Sean was impressed at the professional tone and businesslike manner. Settling back into his seat, he let her work. Relief flooded him as he listened to her handle the call with finesse, even as she grabbed a pen and Post-it from his desk and began scribbling on it.

"Thank you so much for calling, Mr. Sentoal. Let me check the schedule and speak with Mr. Muldoon, then I'll get back to you." A pause and then, "Of course, I'll tell him you said that. I'm certain he'll be pleased to know you admire his program so much."

Quietly Sean got up and strode across the room to a coat rack by the front door where he grabbed an old faded flannel shirt. He could hear Shannon behind him wrapping up the phone call as he put it on.

"You have a lovely evening now, Paul. Good-bye."

If she could work a computer half as well as she just managed one of the biggest names in the horseracing business, then his problems were most definitely solved. No more phones. No more spreadsheets that made his head want to explode.

His mind made up, Sean said over his shoulder, "Anybody who can handle a phone call with one of the most cantankerous old farts you'll ever meet and ends up on first-name basis by the end gets my vote. You're hired. Now come away with me and I'll show you around."

Spinning slowly around, Sean stopped when he caught a glimpse of her expression. She was staring hard at his chest with a frown. "What?" he asked, wondering if he'd left his fly down or something else dumb like that.

"You're wearing flannel."

He cocked a jet-black brow. "And?"

"My sister hates it."

Sean shot her a grin and strode out the door, his voice trailing after him. "That's only because she hasn't seen me in it."

He could hear scuffling behind him as she hurried to catch up. "I'm sure I didn't hear that right. What did you say?"

She glanced up when she reached his side, and their gazes locked. For a moment his brain went fuzzy, like a radio station going out of tune. Then it snapped back, crystal clear. Just like nothing had happened. Warm, rich pools of brown looked expectantly back at him, all soft and innocently seductive. And his brain went fuzzy again. He shook his head, frowning. It had to be her eyes. There was something about them.

He spoke quietly, "I said, 'come.'"

As soon as he said those words, something deep in him stirred restlessly to life. And by her quick intake of breath, she felt something too.

For some reason that made him smile.

Chapter Three

ANY FLEDGLING BIT of confidence Shannon had managed to gain just took a nosedive and crash landed in a pile of smoke. How was she going to save her family now?

She wouldn't—not if she kept panicking, which she was prone to do.

She was so screwed. Royally, totally, *completely* screwed. Why on earth did Sean Muldoon have to go and be the sexiest freaking man alive? Like, the absolute *sexiest*. What had she ever done to deserve this?

Cruel, stupid world.

How was she supposed to pull off this stealth mission and find dirt on the guy if she couldn't see past her own hormones long enough to snoop? And seriously, what could be more unfair than for such a bad person to look so, so ridiculously good?

I said come.

The words echoed in the pit of her stomach as she followed behind him and tried very hard not to check him out. Had she imagined the double entendre? *Ugh.* If she had, then maybe there was something to all the stuff Colleen had said. Maybe she did need to get laid.

A vivid image of sweaty, tangled naked limbs popped into her head before she knew it and she nearly gasped. Not so much at the mental picture itself, but at the subjects who were twisted up like a folded slinky. It was seeing the Irishman striding so confidently down the stable corridor in front of her, with his impressively muscled broad shoulders and tight backside—and having the image of them inside her mind, sans clothing.

Even as she took a steadying breath for composure, her heart rate sped up and she could feel heat flooding her cheeks. If he looked over his shoulder at her right now, she'd probably have "I'm picturing you naked!" stamped across her forehead. She was so guilty.

But man, she had to give her imagination credit. *Damn.*

Maybe she'd gone off the deep end from all the pressure being put on her to save the family's farm. She was broken. And this was the result. Her brain had split and the only neurons making any connections from one side to the other were the horny ones.

Sounded plausible, didn't it? Maybe she should go ask Colleen. *Now.*

"I need to pee!" Shannon blurted out frantically.

One part of her brain registered that she was dangerously close to sounding like a crazy person, but she didn't care. Her chest had gone tight like a clamped vice and she was struggling to breathe.

It had been years since she'd had a full-blown panic attack, but she recognized the telltale signs of one beginning now. What she needed were a few minutes in a quiet place to calm down and get a hold of herself. If she'd declared that need rather ineptly, it couldn't matter. Not when the alternative was hyperventilating until she passed out.

"The toilet is over there," he said, oh so calm. If the guy was weirded out by her odd behavior, he certainly didn't show it. Not that it mattered really, in that moment.

Following in the direction he'd pointed, Shannon choked out a garbled, "Thank you!" and dashed past a large tack room and then cut a hard right. Directly ahead was a door with a hand-carved wooden sign on it that read BATHROOM. Scrambling through, she kicked it shut, flung her back up against it, and barely registered the sparse and rustic surroundings while she frantically fought for breath.

How could her father put her up to something like this and expect her to *actually* go through with it?

Worry seized her and had her hard in its grip while she gasped for air; her lungs squeezed so tight it felt almost an impossible task. All the ramifications and potential consequences of what she was doing came crashing down on her, had her fighting back tears and biting her trembling bottom lip. She couldn't just *ruin* a person's life. What kind of monster would that make her?

Shannon looked up and saw her reflection in the mirror above the sink directly across from her. The state of shock and helplessness that she registered in her expression brought tears flooding down her cheeks, hot and furious all at once.

Why did fixing her family's problems always have to fall on her shoulders?

It was so much *pressure*.

A solid, thudding knock on the door directly behind her head scared the crap out of her and she jumped away from the door, her heart palpitating wildly. "Are you well, Shannon?" came Sean's deep, rich timbre through the barrier.

Swiping clumsily at the tears streaking her cheeks, she gulped a great breath of air and managed to reply weakly, "I'm fine," and then an even less convincing, "Really."

"Why don't you come on out here and let me have a look at you?"

God, that's about the last thing in the world she needed right now—for Sean to see her face all puffy and blotchy from crying. Shaking her head like he could magically see through the pine plank door at her, Shannon replied more steadily this time, "I'm fine, truly. Just tired from all the travel, that's all." Maybe if she repeated that like a mantra in her head for the next decade or two, she could make it true.

Shannon was unsure of the cause, but slowly she felt the tension starting to ease from her body as the panic began to recede. Whether the attack was running its course or talking to Sean had distracted her out of it, she couldn't tell. All she knew was that she was thankful that it was almost over.

And deeply unsettled that they had returned.

For three years she'd been attack free—almost cured of her anxiety disorder. Three full years of carefully cultivated peace. Hours of managing and maintaining her life in as stress- and anxiety-free an environment as she could make it. And it had worked well, keeping the major panic attacks at bay and leaving only the mild day-to-day anxiety, which hummed like white noise in the back of her mind.

Instead of living in the guest house on her parents' property like they'd wanted, she had her apartment just off Broadway in Saratoga Springs that she loved more than anything. She had her Swedish Warmblood jumping horse, Teddy, who was like her baby and whom she adored to bits—and whom she kept stabled at another farm so that she didn't have to constantly see and deal with her family. She'd learned to avoid situations that knowingly spiked her levels, and time together with her mother and father was a biggie.

What happened to parents recognizing their child's autonomy and treating them with respect? She was coming up on thirty next year, and as much as she tried to convince them otherwise, they refused to acknowledge that she was a completely separate person from them. And now, here she was, reduced to panic attacks again, with all her hard work down the drain because she'd failed to stand up to her father and say no when she should have.

But saying no meant damning her entire family to a sad existence, and he knew she was far too loyal to let them suffer when she had the ability to do something about it. Her father knew it—he'd exploited it.

And he'd won.

Shannon straightened her shoulders and brushed back loose strands of hair with shaking fingers. Colleen was her best friend as well as her sister, and she had her whole future ahead of her—one that included being a brilliant doctor out saving the world one patient at a time. She deserved this, if no one else in her family did. And as much as a part of Shannon wished that Colleen had been chosen instead of her, it simply hadn't been an option. For one, her sister couldn't keep a secret if the world depended on it. God, no. She was far too blunt and honest—and had zero tact. And for two, she was about to start rotations at a teaching hospital in Cambridge and her stress level was through the roof, making her even more brash than normal. As much as Shannon loved her, the woman simply lacked the ability to be discreet.

Shannon, however, could be discreet as a field mouse. It came from years of sitting down and shutting up like a good little girl. Disappearing into the floor had been her specialty.

Feeling resolve settle over her, Shannon wiped at her cheeks again and puffed out a breath. "I can do this," she said quietly into the small room. This was for her sister. For Colleen's future.

Raising her hand in a half-hearted cheer of fist pumping to bolster her confidence, she was just about to open the door and step out to do this thing when her phone began to vibrate in her pocket. Startled, Shannon grabbed it quickly and opened the screen with a touch and swipe of her thumb.

It was a text from her father with one single demand:

Secure the position.

And then just as she'd finished scanning the first message, another one came through. Even as anxiety began to creep its ugly, sneaky little self back up her spine, she pulled up the new message and read:

Remember what's at stake.

How could she possibly forget? Even if she wanted to, he wouldn't let her. God, no wonder she'd had an ulcer on and off since she was fifteen. He was *such* a loving paternal figure. It was almost impossible for her to believe that once, long ago in the recesses of her childhood, he'd been a different man—a loving one. For about the millionth time, she wondered what the hell had happened.

"Shannon?" came her name once more, soft and lyrical through the door. There was such genuine concern expressed in those two syllables that it set off a sharp, poignant pang deep in her chest that brought tears back to her eyes. Blinking hard, she glanced down at her smartphone screen to where her father's ominous warning glared back at her, so domineering and grave, and she let out an unsteady breath.

Whatever connection she'd just felt between her and Sean had to be irrelevant. She had to pretend like it hadn't happened at all to begin with. Because as much as she hated being bullied by her father, the truth was that she loved him and her family that much more.

Straightening her back once more with all the resolve she could muster, Shannon brushed her braid back and gripped the doorknob, prepared to open the door.

Piece of cake. No big thing. A total and complete walk in the park.

All that bolstering worked until she swung the door open and got a good look at Sean Muldoon's face. Her ability to put coherent thought together disseminated into a thousand useless pieces. Green eyes as clear and bold as her collection of decorative glass looked at her with genuine concern and kindness.

She didn't know what to make of it, so she downplayed and hoped beyond hope that her crying jag wasn't as obvious as she was pretty sure it was. "Sorry about that. It seems that I'm more worn out than I realized." When his gaze stayed level with hers and he didn't crack so much as a fraction of a smile, she tried for a joke. "That, or the airport food in Newark is suspect."

The corners of his finely sculpted lips finally curled upward in a small, lopsided smile and her stomach went all excited and jittery. It really wasn't fair that he was so good looking. It was all that Black Irish that was so evident in him, giving him golden skin, coal-black hair, and those wild green eyes. That, combined with his tall, muscular body and rugged demeanor (the crescent-shaped scar on his chin helped with that too), made it fair to say that the guy was pretty much the perfect amalgam of every man, factual or imaginary, that she'd ever lusted after.

"Let's do the tour later, shall we?" he said and took a step closer. Shannon could feel his energy brush against her, and her pulse quickened in response. He was just so masculine. For goodness' sake, he even *smelled* male. Like earth and pine and clean soap.

Feeling her brain start to melt at his nearness, she was completely unprepared when he reached out and cupped her chin with a huge, work-hardened hand. Though his hands were rough, his touch was light and gentle. "You look worked, lass. Some rest will set you to right again. We'll pick this up again tomorrow."

Shocked by her body's response to his unexpected touch, Shannon could only mutter, "Okay."

His smile grew, revealing slight dimple creases in his stubbled cheeks. "Great, let's get you settled. I hope you don't mind living above the horses. The manager's flat mentioned in the ad is here in the stables, on the top floor at the far end."

"That's fine," she mumbled absently, completely transfixed by the heat of his fingers on her skin and the deep emerald flecks in his eyes. The accent was one seriously seductive bonus.

"Anything you need, tell me, and I'll have it scrounged up for you. You're saving me from the fecking computer." He grinned lightning fast and seductive as fine chocolate—and her brain blew a fuse. "For you, Shannon, there's nothing I won't do."

Chapter Four

THE NEXT AFTERNOON Sean slowed his truck as a bend in the mountain road up ahead came into view. His new stable manager was firmly lodged in his thoughts, making it hard to concentrate on the windy route. What was he supposed to make of Shannon?

He didn't know.

But he *really* wanted to make her naked. And honestly, that's what had him reeling. The reactions and feelings that she evoked in him were disconcerting to say the least. Mostly because he'd never felt anything quite like them before. And maybe more importantly, simply because he couldn't do a damn thing about them.

But feck it all, he was getting really sick of sitting on the sidelines, waiting.

Always waiting. When was he going to be free to live his life, to pursue the things his heart really needed?

Probably never.

His mouth tightened and his hands gripped the wheel hard, frustration and something almost like despair swirling greasily in his gut. Would that answer ever change? Would he ever be free?

Probably not.

Sean thumped the wheel with the heel of his palm, cursing his life in Gaelic before easing into the set of hairpin turns that twisted tightly and then eventually dropped down the mountainside into Glacier Valley, where his adopted hometown of Fortune lay nestled. Founded as an early mining camp by gold panners in search of that ever-elusive shimmering nugget, and then almost immediately abandoned for locales untold, his beloved town had a colorful past that it chose to celebrate and embrace.

Now Sean's adopted home was a thriving, bustling village full of character and quirks and an underbelly of true grit—which he related to and respected. He liked that he'd picked a home-away-from-home that had clawed its way from neglect and transformed itself into something with substance. He liked to think that it said a little something about himself that he'd chosen such a place to call his own.

His first real home.

Sighing as the view pulled on his heartstrings, Sean noticed that Jasper's Peak was still capped in glistening snow even though it was June. Jesus, that sight would never get old. Whatever the season or weather, that jagged mountain was spectacular as it stood sentry over the valley at its feet. It had called to him when he'd first stumbled into town—that sense of protection and safety he'd felt from it.

It's why he'd stayed five years ago, instead of moving on.

At that time, all he'd wanted was a quiet place to hunker down and hide out until the storm passed. That *storm* being a mob-initiated manhunt for him over a bet gone horribly wrong.

He'd warned Mickey O'Banion not to place wagers on him when the short, stocky mobster had come into the back room of Flannery's Pub. The Russian boxer his manager had just secured him a match with was out of Sean's league and he knew it. Bigger than him by fifty pounds of rock-hard muscle, with more experience and a lot of shite for brains, that big bastard was crazy *and* dumb. A deadly combination, to be sure.

Sean had assured O'Banion he was deeply flattered and appreciative of his admiration, but tried to impress on him that it was in his own best interest to not throw pounds down on the match. Sean had always been honest about his abilities, and this was one time in which he knew he was in over his head. Unfortunately for him, there'd been no way to back out—not with all the betting money being flung around. He'd had a lot of people to make good for then—and felt every ounce of the pressure.

But the white-haired mob boss with the deceptively cordial manner had declared bollocks on Sean's protests, claiming his worries were nothing more than performance anxiety. As evidence of his considerable arrogance and overinflated confidence, Mickey declared that he was so certain of Sean's success in the ring that in addition to his original wager, he would separately bet Sean his prize new bay Thoroughbred—a foal that he'd just acquired from the finest horseracing farm in Ireland—against the odds of Sean losing out to a foreigner.

Sean had protested with all his might, knowing full well who O'Banion was and wanting nothing to do with him. It was a well-known fact on the streets of Dublin that being involved in a bet with the mob was about the stupidest thing in the world a person could do. Because no matter which way the bet went, the person was screwed and almost always wound up floating face down in a river.

The Irish mob took their betting seriously. It was some sort of twisted code of honor that they believed the bet had to be completed. It was only *after* the competition was over and they'd honored their fecked-up code that they could kill him and take the horse back with a clear conscience.

And Sean, well, he very much liked being alive.

He'd hemmed, he'd protested—he'd all but begged O'Banion not to bet his horse that night in Flannery's Pub. But in the end, he'd found himself deep in their twisted trap anyway. Refusing hadn't been an option for Sean, not since he'd wanted to keep his hands attached to his body at least long enough to box the Russian. But then he'd lost the boxing match like he'd predicted he would, thereby winning the bet, and he wound up the reluctant owner of a colt—which he didn't have a clue what to do with—and a death warrant. But he'd kept his hands and his life, and that had meant everything.

He'd spent the evening after the fateful exchange scrambling for the quickest passage out of the country: a cargo ship that had agreed to transport him and the colt for cold, hard cash. Sean had gratefully given all he had, and then waited three terrifying hours for the ship to undock. He'd passed that time in a nearby pub at the bottom of a shot glass of Irish whiskey, mourning the state of his life.

His life was now a slowly sifting hourglass? *Nah.*

In the end it had been Garth Brooks and his friends in low places who'd shown Sean the way out of his dire predicament and onto the path that had led to his current life. When that American country-western song had come on the jukebox in the corner of that smoky pub he'd been holed up in, he'd had an important realization: He had a chance to start completely new. To be *anybody.* He'd found inspiration and followed Garth's lead, moving out to the American West with his newly acquired horse to become a rancher, intent on reinventing himself.

And he had.

In more ways than one, he thought as he drove down the bustling Main Street and pulled into the parking lot next to Two Moons Brewery and Pub. The sun was just starting to set behind Jasper's Peak, tinting the sky in wispy shades of violet and rose. Sean knew that if he stood there, in a few more minutes the sun would hit the horizon and the sky would light up, exploding in a glow of bold magentas and orange.

Having that beautiful and colorful display in the sky on a regular basis was something he'd never take for granted, not after decades of Ireland's soggy, cloud-covered evenings. They had a beauty about them all their own, to be sure. But after living in Fortune for over five years now, he'd come to realize just how much he appreciated the dry, clear weather of the Colorado Rockies.

It was uplifting. Uncomplicated. Invigorating.

And it suited him.

Maybe more to the point, it had been what his heart had needed at the time when he'd first arrived. The wide-open expanse of blue sky had spoken to him like nothing else in the world ever could. It still did.

Sean climbed out of his pickup and inhaled the tantalizing aroma of pine, summer flowers, and sun-warmed earth. For a guy who'd grown up in urban Dublin, he'd taken to country life exceptionally fast—like he'd been born for it. The sense of freedom he experienced every day was priceless.

"Sean, my boy. Good to see you!" came a holler from behind him.

Spinning around as he pocketed his keys, Sean grinned when he spotted Gerry Jaffey on the sidewalk. The old man was salty as a sea dog and twice as surly. "And a good day to you!" Sean gestured with a hand toward the pub. "Care to join me for a pint?"

The balding, stooped man shook his head and leaned on his walking cane. "The wife would have my hide if I did. She's worried about my health and has banned me from drinking." His voice grew louder as his sense of indignation bloomed. "Woman ruins all my fun. Have one tiny stroke and you'd think the world had come to an end."

Sean figured that for Gerry's wife, Dolores, her world probably *had* come to an end when he'd stroked. Taking a few steps and reaching out, he patted the old guy's shoulder and joked, "Women. Can't live with 'em, no? Well, if you change your mind, I'll be inside."

"I'll remember that," said Gerry, nodding seriously.

They parted and Sean opened the door to go inside the brewpub, knowing he'd find Jake working behind the bar. His hand was still gripping the old wooden handle when a blur of movement out of the corner of his eye startled him. He looked down just in time to see a short, curvy blonde with big tortoise shell glasses and a high bun dart beneath his arm and swish by him through the open door. Recognizing the town's librarian, Apple Woodman, he smiled widely and let out a laugh because he'd seen the look on her face—it wasn't a happy one. And he knew that there was only one person inside Two Moons who had such a knack for pissing women off like that.

Jake was in big trouble.

Following at a more leisurely pace than the busty librarian's agitated clip, he stopped when he came upon Jake and Apple squaring off at the bar.

"You stood me up!"

"Now, Apple, calm down. I'm really sorry." Jake's deep voice sounded a little strained. Given that he was holding his hands up like she'd yelled "Freeze!" Sean thought it was damn funny to see a white bar towel dangling from his friend's fist like a mini flag of surrender. Whatever he'd done, it had to be bad. He'd known Apple for going on five years now, and he'd never once seen the sweet and shy woman upset like this.

But she was sure pissed now. One hand was planted on her ample hip and the other was raised up with her finger pointed like a laser at Jake's nose. Even Sean felt a little scolded, and he was far outside the line of fire. He chuckled. She was *good*. His mum would have been proud.

"Jake Stone, you…you *scoundrel*. I've been waiting for two hours. *Two whole hours*, and you didn't show! We had an agreement. You *promised*." Her finger began to shake and she chewed her bottom lip before blurting out, "You have no idea what you're doing to me!"

As Sean watched, she burst into tears and then ran out the door, the skirt of her floral print dress flapping and floating wildly around her bare knees. Aidan Booker was just stepping through the door when she charged through and rammed into his side. She mumbled an apology and disappeared onto the sidewalk, then out of sight.

Aidan tipped his head in the direction Apple had gone. "What's the deal with her?" He looked past Sean to where Jake was standing behind the bar with a deep scowl on his face. "What the hell did you do?"

Jake let out a loud sigh and crossed his arms. "Nothing, man. I don't know what's wrong with her." He gave an ill-natured shrug of his broad shoulders. "Okay, so maybe I had told her I'd let her ask me some questions about my family's history for this thing she's writing about Fortune, or something. I don't know. It didn't seem like a big deal and I tried to text her when I couldn't make it. Not my fault if she didn't get it," he finished, grumbling.

Aidan pulled up a plain wooden bar stool and sat down, his tone casual when he asked the very question Sean had been wondering. "So you *did* stand her up, then?"

"Yeah, so what if I did? I had good reason."

Feeling sorry for the girl, but knowing his friend wasn't normally such an arsehole, Sean sat down next to Aidan and glanced around the mostly empty pub. The only other person there besides them was Bart Hoffer, and he was thoroughly engrossed in whatever online thing he was doing with headphones and his computer. He hadn't glanced up once during Apple's outburst, for which Sean was glad, because he liked her. She was a lovely lass and he'd hate for her to feel embarrassed. She was normally so shy as it was. He was a regular user of the library, but he'd never been able to get more than a sentence or two out of her before she started blushing profusely.

"I'd be interested in hearing this reason, mate. That lass looked fair crushed when she ran out of here."

Aidan chimed in, "Yeah, man. She was in bad shape all right." He took a pull from the bottle of ale Jake had just slid down the bar to him, and Sean caught the frown he was trying to hide. But Aidan couldn't quite hide the irritation in his voice when he added, "That *project* of hers that you blew off so casually is the nonfiction book on the history of Fortune that she's under contract with one of the big publishing houses to write. You know, no big deal."

Sean noticed a tick had started under Aidan's right eye. Every time he looked at Jake, it went off. Something about the situation was definitely getting under his skin.

Jake began wiping down the bar and grumbled, "I don't see what that has to do with me."

Aidan jerked in his seat like he'd been poked with an electric cattle prod, his face blank with disbelief. He sputtered, "You, you really don't know?"

Even Sean had to call bollocks on that one. "You know damn well what she's after, Stone." It was his loony family who'd founded Fortune the first time around. "You're just being stubborn." Being obstinate for the fun of it was his forte. Sean snagged the beer bottle Jake had sat in front of him and took a swig, suddenly feeling a little irritated on Apple's behalf too.

Obviously trying to change the subject, the pub owner placed his elbows on the bar top and said, "Have we decided yet if we're going to help host that pet adoption day for Mimi's Animal Refuge that's happening in a few weeks? I just got another call from one of the volunteers." He looked from Aidan to Sean and back, his brown eyes filled with humor. "Honestly, I think it's a great idea for the Bachelors of Fortune to be available for autographs. It'll draw people out to the event, and God knows those pets deserve families."

Stubborn Jake might be, but the guy was mush when it came to animals. Especially ones in need. "I'm willing, if you two are," Sean said.

"I'm okay with it. It's the least we can do for being such lucky bastards," Aidan chimed in. "I might even land a date."

Not that any of them had had a problem getting dates, particularly. Not since the day the three of them had struck gold in the river behind Jake's cabin. Overnight their lives had changed. One day they'd been just three best friends, regular guys who, after testing out one of Jake's homebrew recipes and getting pissed as the wind, had decided it would be fun to try their hand at prospecting. They'd joked that since Jake's place was the area's original homestead and the river behind it the same one his ancestors had panned, maybe they'd get lucky. Little had they expected that to be exactly what occurred.

But it had. And once word got out about their miraculous gold strike, they became local celebrities, the regional papers and media outlets eating up their story like candy. In no time, they'd been dubbed the Bachelors of Fortune and had gained a public following—mostly single women. Now they were often asked to make appearances together, like this adoption event. The three of them figured it was the least they could do. Kind of like paying it forward for getting so damn lucky.

Still, though he never admitted it, having a public presence made Sean uneasy. And, well, sometimes those women could be so pushy and enthusiastic that it was a little scary. He remembered a particular incident when one woman followed him into the bathroom there at the pub and flashed him her boobs. It hadn't been pretty. She hadn't been wearing a bra.

And she'd been like, eighty.

He cringed at the memory. "When are we going to stop being called the Bachelors of Fortune, anyway? Shouldn't our popularity be waning? Besides, I've got better things to do with me time than fending off desperate females only out for a poke and a chance at me cash." Just the thought made Sean shudder. Days of meaningless sex with nameless, faceless women were so far in his past. And he was glad for it.

Jake cracked a grin as he dried a pint glass with his towel. "It's what you get for being so damned charming."

He chuckled and said to his friends, "Speaking of charms, your plan to find me a stable manager worked out beautifully in my favor today."

Jake's gaze whipped up and he looked across the bar at Aidan. "See? I told you he wouldn't be pissed about it forever, man."

Aidan shook his head, openly disagreeing. "I know that it's natural behavior for you, but I didn't want to overstep my bounds, is all."

Jake didn't rise to the bait, only grinned and replied, "Why not? It makes life way more fun and interesting." He dismissed Aidan and turned to look at Sean, his brown eyes full of curiosity. "So who'd you hire? Was it Bryan Harding from the feed co-op? I heard he was looking for work the other day when I had breakfast at the Claim Jumper Cafe. Joe Sherman told me over biscuits and gravy."

An image of Shannon flashed through Sean's mind again, looking all sexy and warm with her down-to-earth sensuality. Heat bloomed gently in his chest and his pulse picked up pace. A feeling began to surface, one that made him uncomfortable because the echo of it felt a lot like yearning or longing or something somewhere in his gut, so he clamped down hard on the emotion and rejected it outright. But he couldn't stop the warm, fuzzy feeling that had taken up residence right in the center of his chest at the mental image of his new stable manager.

Aidan kicked the bottom rung of his bar stool, jarring him from his thoughts. "Hey, Muldoon. Who'd you hire?"

Sean reached for the bottle of Jake's signature brew and brought it to his lips. Before he took a drink, he said quietly, "Her name is Shannon." He smiled briefly, secretively, before taking a good long sip of the craft beer. Jesus, even just saying her name was satisfying.

For a guy with an uncertain future who had nothing to give a lady, that could potentially be a problem.

At that moment, something caught his attention and he swiveled his head, startled. A reflection rippled in the large pub window directly across the bar from him, there one minute and gone the next. It lasted just long enough to give an impression of menacing dark eyes and blunt, ugly features. His throat instantly went tight and he wheezed, caught completely off guard by a surge of fear that had come out of nowhere.

Feck! It couldn't be. He thought that guy was dead.

Sean zeroed in on the spot where he could swear he'd just seen someone from his past, hoping if he stared hard enough the reflection would magically reappear and he could know for sure.

But there was no one there.

Did dead men walk?

Aidan spoke. "Hey. You all right, man? You look like you've just seen a ghost." His mate eyed him with concern before following Sean's gaze to the empty window, frowning with confusion. "What's got you spooked?"

Inhaling a steadying breath, Sean counted to three and then blew it out slowly, encouraging his body to relax. Instead of answering, though, he asked his own question. "Did either of you see anything in that window just now?"

Jake tossed him a curious look, his eyes narrowing suspiciously. "That depends. What am I supposed to have seen?"

For a bloody bartender, the guy was too fecking perceptive for his own good. Deciding to err on the side of truth, Sean replied with forced casualness as he scanned the brewpub. "A bloke I used to know back in Dublin."

Jake's look was deadpan. "That's not helpful."

"Fine. He's an ugly bugger." He held a hand up to his face, his palm flat on the tip of his nose. "Flat, almost shapeless nose, blunt features. Big head. Beady, small dark eyes." Still feeling a little shaky and wondering more than a little about the state of his sanity, Sean reached for his ale. It helped to have something constructive to do with his hands, a way to diffuse the nervous energy.

Aidan chuckled. "Sounds like a real looker. Too bad I didn't see him."

Pulling a pint from tap, Jake shook his head. "Sorry, man. I didn't see anyone who looked like that. By the way you're sitting all tense though, I'm guessing this isn't somebody you were friends with?"

Sean thought back to the last time he'd seen Billy Hennessey. It hadn't been Hennessey's finest moment.

Nor had it been his, honestly. Being scared for one's life didn't typically bring out the best in them. "You could say he's got a grudge against me." If he was still alive, that was.

Both Aidan and Jake asked at the same time, "Why?"

Sean smirked despite himself. "Because I'm the one who gave him the fecked-up face."

"No shit?" asked Jake, his eyes bright with interest. "You two got in a fist fight? Was this one of your commissioned matches you used to fight or a personal thing?"

"It was personal."

"Yeah?" Aidan added. "Did you kick his ass?"

Talking to them was helping Sean calm down. It was reassuring that they hadn't seen anything, especially since Jake had been facing the window, too. If Hennessey had been there, no doubt his mate would have seen him. Jesus, maybe he was just being paranoid.

Because those two were like family, he divulged a little more truth. "I did kick his arse, actually."

That was putting it gently—sugarcoating it, for sure. The truth was, the last time he'd seen Hennessey had been directly after his fight with the crazy Russian. He'd just come to again after being knocked out hard. He'd opened a swollen eye to discover the place quiet and still, except for the confusing sound of a horse nickering softly somewhere nearby. Lying face down on the cold concrete floor of the old abandoned warehouse he'd fought in, which had recently been brimming with spectators, he'd tried to gain his bearings. Why was the place empty? How long had he been unconscious? His body bruised and aching profusely, Sean had blinked to clear his blurred vision when a shadow fell over him. Hennessey hooked a booted foot under him, rolling him over.

Crouching down next to him, the hit man had smiled as he stroked the flat of a knife blade against his cheek, a crazed light in his dark eyes. "Ye just made me day, bugger squat."

His mouth dry as dust and his ribcage screaming in agony, Sean had whispered raggedly, "How?" Had the thug bet against him?

Hennessey reached out a meaty, stubby-fingered hand and brushed back a clump of sweat- and blood-matted hair covering Sean's eyes; the gesture had been weirdly kind and maternal for a cold-blooded killer. "Because ye lost, lovey." He tipped his head toward the far corner. "See yer prize?"

"What prize?" Sean asked weakly, his brain struggling to make sense of things.

"Why, yer new racehorse, of course! Ye won him fair and O'Banion's already paid up. Look," Hennessey said, grabbing Sean's chin and forcing him to see the bay colt that stood restlessly, nervously in the corner, as his nostrils flared. "Ain't he a beauty?" He'd stared at Sean, his expression almost childlike and innocent.

"I don't want him," Sean had protested instantly.

Hennessey laughed. "Too bad, a bet's a bet. And now that the boss has made good on his end, it's my turn with ye."

Dread had curdled Sean's blood, making him queasy. "What's that mean?"

Suddenly Hennessey had contorted and he'd spat in Sean's face, rising to his feet with the big knife clenched in his fist. "That yer the mouse and I'm the fecking anaconda. Yer dead already. Ye better feckin' run, Donaghy."

One glimpse in the hit man's abnormally bright eyes, devoid of any sanity, and fear had flooded Sean. On a surge of adrenaline, he had lashed out a hand, grabbing the thug's ankle and pulling him clean off his feet. Hennessey released a sound of surprise and fell hard, hitting the ground with a grunt. Taking advantage of the moment, Sean had lunged after him.

Riding on panic and knowing he was fighting for his very life, he'd climbed on the cold-blooded murderer and begun slamming his fists into his face. Over and over and over. He couldn't think. Could barely see. He'd just kept punching until he felt bone crush beneath his hand and blood spewed from Hennessey's nose. Then he swung some more, not stopping even when the hit man went limp. He didn't stop until the sound of hooves clapping sharply against concrete registered in his panicked brain and he looked up to see that the colt had moved close and was standing over them, wide-eyed and snorting softly.

Sean had looked from the horse down to the prone mobster, one of his hands fisted and frozen in midswing. He couldn't tell if Hennessey was still breathing. Maybe he was dead; maybe he'd killed him with his bare hands.

With that new fear riding him, Sean had climbed off the hit man with terrible, shaking legs, his mind confused and reeling. Without thought and without knowing why, he'd grabbed the colt's lead rope and stumbled out of the abandoned warehouse into the night, the young horse following obediently.

Then they'd run.

Coming back to the present, Sean shook his head to clear it and sighed, feeling heavy. He'd thought his days of running were behind him. Prayed they were. Maybe he'd just been fooling himself.

"At any rate, I'm probably imagining things," he said to the guys finally, not wanting them to worry. Besides, this wasn't the first time he'd imagined seeing Hennessey. It wasn't even the fifth or the tenth. Maybe, just for kicks, his recurring nightmare that starred the hit man and woke him in cold sweats was finally permeating his waking hours too.

It was either that or the past was really catching up to him. Sean glanced once more to the window where he thought he'd seen Hennessey's reflection.

Shite.

He hoped like hell he was just going crazy.

Chapter Five

SHANNON WOKE THE next morning with two distinct thoughts in her head, the first being how in the heck she was going to pull off this scheme like her father expected her to, and the second being decidedly R-rated and involving mentally rehashing the sexiness factor of Sean Muldoon.

Off. The. Charts.

Rolling onto her back and covering her eyes with a forearm, she sighed heavily at the unfairness of it all. But of course, it fit right in line with everything in her life always being so much more complicated than necessary. Why wouldn't the bad guy she was sent to spy on have a megawatt smile sexy enough to start her undercarriage steaming? Yes—in *that* way.

Last time she'd even felt the temperature rise down there had been a few years ago when she'd watched one of the Avengers movies and become transfixed by

Captain America's chest-hugging uniform as he battled the naughty Norse god Loki all over New York City and back. Now *that* was quality entertainment.

But this, this instantaneous attraction she felt for Sean, was unreal. And completely unacceptable. Just because his eyelashes rivaled Ian Somerhalder's and he had an ass as firm and round as a juicy apple (yes, she'd had the desire to bite it just like one, too) *and* she'd had all kinds of wild dreams about him last night didn't mean she could do anything about it.

Even if she did have the nerve—or the blind stupidity— to go and jump his bones like she'd dreamt last night, there were still the unwelcome facts of the situation: Sean Muldoon was putting her parents out of business. She was only there to learn how and find a way to stop him. It didn't matter what her personal feelings about the subject were. It never did.

Kicking off her covers, Shannon climbed out of bed, anxiety immediately by her side and making her mad. God, she was so sick of it—*all* of it! The overbearing, hearing-impaired parents, the anxiety issues, the constant feeling of dread she'd dragged around with her since the moment her father made saving the family business and legacy *her* responsibility.

This was the last straw. After this, she was done blindly doing what she was told. Done letting others push her around. It was time for a whole new Shannon—a brave one.

And the new her was finally going to grab the courage to open her own riding school for children like she'd always wanted to as soon as she got back to Saratoga. No more Grand Prix. She'd never loved it anyway. No more denying her needs in favor of everyone else's and putting off her happiness for tomorrow.

No. More.

She was ready to be happy *today*.

Pushing at the mess of hair that half-covered her face, Shannon grumbled about the state of her life as she padded barefoot across the old plank wood floor of her new abode. As much as she'd been prepared not to like the stable manager's studio loft above the barn, she'd taken one look and fallen in love. Against her better judgment, of course. Still, it had been impossible not to when she'd opened the door to a light-filled apartment with a vaulted exposed-beam ceiling, panoramic window that took up the entire far wall and overlooked the most spectacular mountains she'd ever seen, and deep-cushioned furniture in faded denim blue covers.

But her favorite thing of all was the shortened picnic table somebody had painted brick red, and turned into a small, four-seat dining table. A bunch of the white lilacs she'd seen blooming on bushes near the driveway would look gorgeous on it, if she could find a vase. There had to be something she could use to put them in around somewhere. She could already smell their heavenly sweet scent and smiled in anticipation.

Feeling her spirits lift and noting how her earlier anxiety was dissipating, Shannon congratulated herself on being able to move away from her troubling thoughts before they began looping in her brain over and over like a broken record player, driving her crazy.

Without her parents' knowledge, she'd started seeing a therapist for her anxiety issues about six months ago. They'd spiked hard after she'd failed to place in the Grand Prix finals, and her parents hadn't held back on letting her know how much she'd disappointed them. Being kind to herself and self-congratulatory when she'd stemmed off an attack might seem the obvious and healthy response, but for someone raised with constant criticism being flung her way, it was often difficult to do. Her "normal" preprogrammed response was to criticize herself and find flaws because her parents had. If they weren't there to do it, she would—and did.

But all that was changing, one staved-off anxiety attack at a time.

Shannon's cell phone began ringing on the counter in the small kitchenette where she'd left it.

"Shit!" she exclaimed.

Suddenly apprehensive, she hustled to it and snatched it up off the faded yellow Formica countertop, noting that it was her father on the caller ID. "Hello, Dad," she said a little breathlessly, her heart beginning to beat faster.

"Why didn't you call me last night?" he demanded.

No hello back, no asking how she was doing, no sentiment of concern for her well-being whatsoever. So frigging typical. She was beginning to wonder at the futility of her parents ever seeing her for who she was and showing her any warmth and affection. At the rate things were going, she'd be waiting her entire lifetime.

God, at this point, was it even worth it anymore?

She rolled her eyes to the pine-beam ceiling and prayed for her trusty patience. "My apologies. It turned out to be a more tiring day than I expected and I fell asleep early. It's inexcusable, I know—and I'm sorry." The only way to pacify her father when he was angry and feeling thwarted was with apologies. And she was so accustomed to that being his expectation that she'd managed to do it twice before she caught herself and stopped.

Wait a minute. What did she have to apologize for? For being exhausted after a rough day and falling asleep?

Screw that.

Right?

It took a whole lot of nerve for her to do it, but she cut him off before he could berate her any further and took control of the conversation by stating, "I have the job and I'm living on the property. Give me a few days to look around and I'll get back to you." And now her knees were wobbly, but she kept going. "Aside from looking for evidence of steroid abuse, is there something I should be searching out?"

With his deep, cultured voice, her father huffed into the receiver and replied stiffly, "Scan his ledgers, his books, his horses' pedigree documents. Go through his home and private effects. You'll find something. This bastard Irishman is dirty, I know it."

Something in the tone of his voice didn't seem right, but she tried to shrug it off. There was a lot at stake. Everyone was tense. "What if I don't find anything, Dad? What if Muldoon is on the up-and-up?" The first question filled her with dread, but the second had something resembling hope trying to find a place to land inside her. She refused to stop and consider why she had that response. Some things just weren't going to happen and thinking about it only gave it false traction, so she just wasn't going to go there.

What did it matter if Sean was legit or not anyway?

"That man is crooked as Bonnie and Clyde, I tell you. You *will* find something." The subsequent *or else* was unspoken yet implied, and hung heavily in the air between them.

One of these days she wouldn't be so worried about his response and possible rejection, and she would stand up to his bullying. Until then, as much as it pained her to admit the truth, she wanted to make her parents proud of her again. Ever since she had tanked at the Grand Prix finals, they'd barely even looked her in the eye—and when they did it was always with censure. They acted like she'd shamed the entire family name.

It was unfair and hurtful.

Yet they were her parents and she loved them. And she wasn't ready to completely give up hope of a better relationship with them—a more equal one. Because of that tiny thread she still clung to, Shannon fisted a hand in her hair and said quietly into the phone, "I'll do my best."

Callum Charlemagne replied matter-of-factly, "I know you will. That's why I chose you instead of your sister."

Great. She had the world on her shoulders because she was the good girl. Could that *be* any more fabulous?

"I remember what a sweet little girl you used to be," he said suddenly, breaking the awkward silence, and Shannon jerked in surprise. "You were always so eager to please your mother and me, so loving. Your sister was always willful and headstrong. But you, you were such a dutiful girl."

Was the man sick or something? He was *never* sentimental.

The last time he'd called her sweet, she'd been ten and had just given him a handmade card she'd worked all day on proclaiming him the best father in the whole big wide world. He'd looked at the pink construction paper with the lopsided Earth and the two figures holding hands that stood on top and said with a genuine smile, "My sweet Shannon. I love it. Thank you." Then he'd wrapped her up in a tight, heartfelt hug before leaving on a month-long business trip to Ireland.

A pang resonated in her heart, the sudden memory both unexpected and deeply poignant. How could she have forgotten that day? It was the last time she'd seen him genuinely smile. But it reminded her that once upon a time he'd been a good father to her, a kinder one. Whatever had caused him to change? He'd once acted like he loved her. But because she still loved him and deep down held the hope that they could *all* be happy again, she took a steadying breath, determining to keep trying.

They stiffly said their good-byes, as though neither really knew what to say after his uncharacteristic display of affection, and hung up. Shannon was just setting the phone down when it started ringing again. This time it was Colleen.

As soon as she picked up, her sister exploded. "Oh my God, have you met him yet?"

Shannon assumed she was referring to Sean. "As a matter of fact, I have."

"He is scrumptious, that man." Big dreamy sigh.

"I wasn't prepared," she had to admit.

"*Now* do you see why I told you to use the ladies? You need to get him naked."

Leave it to her sister to cut to the chase and say the one thing she'd spent the majority of her night dreaming about doing. "I'm not interested."

"Bullshit," her sister scoffed.

Even she didn't buy it, but she still gave it another try, "No, really, I'm not. And besides, even if I was, there's no way I could sleep with him. It's way too complicated."

"What's so complicated about sex?" Colleen demanded, sounding genuinely confused. "You have an itch, you scratch an itch. Simple as that."

For her sister, yes it was. But for Shannon, she'd never been good at casual sex. Emotions always ended up just as tangled as bed sheets. "I don't work like you, Leenie. You're so damn rational and practical that I think you got double your share, plus some."

The line was silent for a heartbeat and then a no-nonsense, "Think about it."

Like there was even a remote chance that she wouldn't. *Please.*

"I'll think about it," she conceded, and was surprised at the butterflies that launched in her belly at the words.

"Oh! I almost forgot to tell you, but when I met him he was wearing a flannel shirt."

Colleen swore once, hard and sharp. "Damn it, why'd you have to go and tell me that? Now he's ruined for me, Shannon! Simply ruined."

"I'm going to laugh my butt off when the man who finally wins your heart is a flannel shirt lover."

"There's a far better chance of you landing between the sheets with the Irish dreamsicle than there is of *any* plaid-wearing guy stealing my heart. No doubt."

Shannon had a sudden thought as she crossed the great room to peruse the view outside. The early morning light that bathed the Rockies took her breath away. "Hey, why are you so keen on me and Muldoon knocking boots when he's the reason our family is in so much trouble anyway?"

Colleen's sigh was deep and long-suffering. "Be-*cause*, it doesn't change the fact that you deserve to let down your hair and have some fun for once in your life. And, because you're crazy about Irishmen—"

"I'm not!"

But her sister kept right on talking without breaking stride. "I know you are because I read your diary when you were home for winter break your sophomore year of college and you went on and on about the Irish boy in your American History class. The one with the punk mohawk."

Stuck briefly between being horribly offended at the invasion of privacy and amused at the reminder of the monster crush she'd had on that kid, Shannon decided to let it go and ended up chuckling at the memories. So maybe she did have a soft spot for those Irish bad boys. Didn't every woman?

A knock sounded at the front door, and Shannon spun around, surprised. Quickly scanning the room for the time, she found a plain round wall clock in the kitchen. Almost seven in the morning. She couldn't possibly be late for work, could she? She could swear she remembered Sean saying eight.

"I've got to go," she said into the phone. "Love you, talk soon."

She hung up and brushed her hands down her body, trying in vain to make herself presentable. Which was pretty hard to do when she was wearing an enormous gray T-shirt with a picture of Li'l Sebastian from her favorite TV show *Parks and Recreation* on the front. Though she adored last year's birthday gift from Colleen, at that moment she'd have given just about anything to be wearing something that wasn't three sizes too big and hung halfway to her knees, leaving her legs bare and exposed.

The knock came again as she reached the door. Wishing desperately for her comfy and *modest* chenille robe that was back in Saratoga Springs, Shannon swallowed hard and swung the door open.

And came eye-to-chin with one very sexy Irishman.

Shannon blinked hard, twice, trying to clear her vision. Nope, he was still there—and still gorgeous. Tall, dark, and handsome didn't even come close to describing Sean Muldoon framed in the morning light, wearing worn jeans, a faded smoky blue pocket T-shirt, and work boots.

And there she was in nothing but an oversized T-shirt with a miniature pony printed on the front of it and hair that resembled Cousin It tangled around her face. It would have been humiliating if she hadn't scrambled to remind herself why she was there in the first place and that her appearance was the last thing she should be worrying about.

It was working too, until he had to go and smile all crooked and sexy. Then her brain started to get foggy and she lost track of what she'd been thinking. What wasn't she supposed to be worried about again?

"Hello, Shannon. That's a lovely outfit you're wearing there."

Ah, right. There it was. Her appearance.

And she was wrong—knowing that she was there under false pretenses and that Sean might be a bad guy didn't change anything.

It was still humiliating.

Chapter Six

Sean bit the inside of his cheek to keep from laughing, but the look on Shannon's face was priceless and he almost couldn't stop. He'd known it would be a bit of a gamble to knock on her door so early considering she'd been so tired last night, that there was a chance he'd wake her up. Especially since he'd told her not to worry about showing until near eight. But he was in a bind this morning and needed her help.

As he watched Shannon's face change from varying shades of red and pink, he tried hard not to think about the glimpse he'd caught of her very shapely bare legs mere seconds ago. If his memory was correct, her toenails were painted a rosy color. And for some reason, that was really sexy to him.

Oh, for feck's sake. It had been a while since his last partner, but he wasn't that hard up, was he? What was the deal? Why was everything about Shannon sexy to him? Shite, he didn't even know her last name!

Frustration spiked in his chest. He wasn't sure why exactly, but he didn't like realizing how little he knew about her. "What's your last name?" he blurted out, even though she was standing in front of him in a baggy nightshirt and messy hair, with big brown eyes still foggy from sleep. Maybe it was *because* she was standing there all warm and rumpled and groggy that he needed to know something personal about her. The moment felt intimate and close. And it had something, some *feeling*, stirring in his chest around the vicinity of his heart.

"My last name?"

"Yes," he demanded, much more gruffly than he'd intended. He didn't want any damn feelings buzzing around inside him. They made him uneasy. Feelings lead to desire—and desire led to wanting things he couldn't have and just causing him misery.

"It's, umm—" she started to say and crossed her arms, inadvertently jiggling her breasts with the movement. "Char…Charles."

His body reacted swiftly and decisively to the view of her erect nipples pushing against the gray cotton fabric with a hard-on that was almost as sudden as it was unexpected. Before he forgot himself and kissed her senseless like he'd wanted to do since the minute she'd opened the door in her pajamas, Sean coughed to cover the sound of surprise that slipped out. "Why don't you get dressed and meet me at the stallion barn?"

Okay, he'd wanted to kiss her since the minute he'd seen her in his office yesterday. There, he admitted it. Bleedin' fool that he was. Something about Shannon called to him on a primitive level and had him feeling emotions like he hadn't in years. Not since he'd run off to America with a promise of retribution hanging over his head and had given up any and all hope of ever having a normal life filled with everyday simple things like a woman to love. He'd known back then that those things wouldn't be in the cards for him, and he'd accepted that fate.

But ever since that realization, his emotions had simply shut down production, in a lot of ways. Life had stopped having the power to sway him into feeling one way or another and had simply just become, well, *life*. Nothing spectacular, nothing to make him feel a surge of emotion, good or bad. Just an uneventful ride that he made the best of every day.

Until her.

He scanned her face, taking in her delicate features and pretty skin, until he met her gaze and their eyes locked. For moments neither one spoke, the energy around them shifting and becoming charged in the silence. All he wanted to do was bend down and taste her lips, to discover if they were as full and soft as they looked.

Like she'd read his mind, her lips parted, almost as if she was giving him an unspoken invitation, and she breathed in, the sound airy and trembling. Transfixed, Sean didn't realize he'd lowered his head until he bumped her forehead with his hard enough to hurt.

She jerked away, startled, and Sean muttered an apologetic, "Shite, I'm sorry." His head stung and he stepped back, lifting a hand to rub at it.

She took a step back too as she rubbed hers and laughed, though it sounded a bit forced to his ears. "No worries. I'll just, umm…" she gestured over her shoulder toward the rest of her apartment, "You know, get dressed and be down in a few minutes."

Way to be cool, arsehole, Sean thought, embarrassed. "Sure, yes. Good," he muttered, feeling like an idiot. Turning to leave, he remembered his manners and spun back around to ask, "How are you finding the flat. Is it of any use?"

The look she gave him was a mixture of confusion and bemusement. "I'm not exactly sure what you mean, but yes, the apartment is great if that's what you're asking."

He made the mistake of looking into her eyes again. Jesus, they were pretty. "Excellent. Well, I'll meet you down there. It's the smaller red barn to the right of here. That's where I keep my racers. This one is for the mares and foals."

She nodded. "Got it."

Stepping back onto the landing, Sean couldn't help himself and stole one last glance at her lovely legs as she began to turn around. And the desire to feel them wrapped around his waist while he plunged deep into her was so instant and visceral it jarred him. It twisted his gut into a hot ball of need like he'd never experienced before, and had him swearing under his breath, "Feck me." He was responding to her like a horny teenager.

"What was that?" she called out from behind him, the feminine tenor of her voice carrying across the room and feeling like a physical caress to his ears.

Knowing he shouldn't, he shifted subtly and tormented himself with one last glimpse of her shapely legs. He wasn't prepared for lust to kick him square in the gut, nearly buckling his knees when she leaned over the table and the back of her shirt rode up, exposing a good expanse of milky white thigh and a hint of curvy, juicy backside.

"Jesus, Mary, and Joseph," he muttered, even though he'd never been a particularly religious man.

But he was still Irish, and by rights superstitious, so he made a quick sign of the cross anyway—maybe half in the hope that God or Jesus or somebody would help him keep his hands off of her. Because at that particular moment, all he wanted to do was stand behind her and slide his palms slowly up those firm, shapely thighs until he discovered whether or not she had knickers on underneath.

And that was such a bad idea for so many reasons. Not the least of which being that anyone he became involved with became a potential target for the mob too if he was discovered, and his conscience simply wouldn't let him allow that.

But it was beginning to feel like, one way or another, something was going to kill him. Mickey O'Banion, one of the boss's thug hit men—or Shannon's delicious body.

Before he lost willpower and tortured himself with another view of Shannon's legs, he mumbled a quick good-bye and headed down the stairs with one thought on his mind: death by incredibly sexy legs didn't sound nearly as bad as it probably should have.

What the bloody hell was wrong with him?

SHANNON HASTILY DRESSED in her only change of clothes—a pair of jeans and T-shirt—thinking she would need to order some clothes to be delivered there, sooner rather than later. If this plan took more than a few days to execute like she was beginning to worry it would, she'd definitely need a few changes of clothing. She'd wanted to bring more but her father had insisted that she travel as lightly as possible, leaving as little to trace back to the Charlemagne name as she could, even though she'd pointed out the absurdity of worrying over whether or not her Banana Republic jeans could somehow be traced back to him. But he'd flat out insisted, so of course she'd ended up doing what he'd wanted.

After dressing, Shannon pulled her hair back in a quick braid and dashed across the wide-open expanse of grass that separated one barn from the other. The day had dawned clear and sunny, with a gentle breeze rustling the trees in the distance. She'd made it about halfway across when the view opened up for her and her step faltered, forcing her to a stop.

It was exquisite.

Now that she was between the two barns, she could see the property clearly. Right behind the buildings the world opened up. Fields upon fields of split-rail fences sprawled out in a flower-filled meadow that gently down-sloped away from her until it came to an end against a densely tree-covered mountain on the other side. Its main peak jutted high into the deep blue sky and had a small cap of bright white snow on top. And to the left a river flanked the fence line, paralleling it about halfway until it forked left again and wandered down a valley between two pine-covered foothills and disappeared out of sight.

Shannon had never seen anything like it before. The wild beauty was almost overwhelming, it was so bold and dramatic. It called to her in a way that was new but deeply personal. Moved profoundly by the view, tears welled in her eyes and she blinked them back.

Why did this place pull at her emotions so strongly? She almost could swear that something inside of her had said HOME the instant she'd laid eyes on it. But she'd told herself she was simply being silly and fanciful and put it out of her mind. Because it was ridiculous, really. Her home was in Saratoga Springs.

Wasn't it?

Absorbed by the breathtaking view, Shannon didn't hear the person approach until he spoke. "You must be our new stable manager Sean told me about. I'm Tim Hopkins, his yearling trainer."

Bringing her focus back, she smiled and held out a hand to the aging man with the pleasant face and kind eyes. "Nice to meet you, I'm Shannon." Because she'd been wondering it, she gestured around and asked, "I didn't get to see much yesterday after I arrived and I've been wondering: Where the main house?" Though she'd looked when she first arrived yesterday, it had been nowhere she could see.

The trainer smiled and chuckled. "It's not so obvious, is it?" Then he raised a hand and pointed to the thick stand of trees behind her. "It's behind that grove there a ways, tucked out of the way from everything."

Why that was fascinating, she didn't know. But she was intrigued by Sean's choosing to live so privately. If her dad was right, it was because he had something to hide. She would rather like to think he simply preferred some personal space.

Better get on with it then. Assuaging her curiosity about Sean's house was going to have to wait. "It's great to meet you, Tim," she said with a smile intended to be friendly and unassuming. "How about we chat longer over coffee soon and you fill me in on the farm?"

Obviously pleased, he rolled back on the heels of his cowboy boots and grinned. "Sounds great."

Spotting Sean emerging from the stallion barn out of the corner of her eye, Shannon began backing toward him as she bid farewell to her new coworker. "Until then, Tim. See you later." Then she turned around and went to meet up with Sean.

It didn't escape her attention that he looked incredibly comfortable standing there on his property with his feet spread and his arms crossed all casual-like. But he didn't look like any of the horsemen or jockeys she'd grown up around, especially now that he had that wool cap back on.

"Why, don't you look the part?" she blurted out when she reached his side.

His liquid green eyes lit with amusement and he laughed, the sound deep and rich. "Which part would you be referring to?"

Shannon was suddenly exasperated and not sure why, only that everything was different than she'd expected it to be and way more complicated. Maybe that was enough to set her on edge. She exclaimed, "Everything! Your horse farm—*you*."

Creases wrinkled the corners of his unbelievable eyes when he smiled, fast and full of wicked humor. "It's a conundrum, isn't it?"

"Yes! Where I come from, horse farms don't look like sprawling cattle ranches in the mountains, and horsemen don't wear jeans with frayed knees and wool caps—and look all, I don't know, *hot*. They wear baseball caps and cowboy hats and sport gross mustaches—and they certainly don't have a body that's built like yours!" She finished on a high note, completely flabbergasted and just plain in over her head with the whole damn thing.

And then she realized what she'd just said and wanted to find a really big hole to go hide in. Just long enough for her to get over the humiliation. Which shouldn't take long. Only maybe, oh, a year or three.

Next thing she knew, Sean's hand was covering hers and he was tugging her along beside him toward the barn entrance at a pace fast enough to make her jog to keep up. "Just because things look different than you expect, lass, doesn't make them less legitimate, worthy, or good." He came to a stop at the door and said in a tone that was all business. "I've got a meeting in town I have to go to and one of my stable hands called in sick. Normally, you wouldn't have to do this, but there's five stalls inside that are already late for their morning clean and I can't do it."

Good God, was he asking her to do what she thought he was? Teddy's was the only stall she'd ever mucked out in her life! Not that she was squeamish or considered herself elitist given her family, but there'd been some things she was happy to pay her horse's boarding farm to do, and shoveling out poop was one of them.

Wanting to protest, but knowing she couldn't, Shannon brushed past him and entered the clean, simple wooden barn with its row of stalls on each side. "No problem," she boasted and grabbed a pitchfork that was leaning against the wall by a bale of hay, inhaling the familiar scent. "It's what I'm here for."

He smiled and her insides turned to jelly. "Great. It's those five stalls behind you there. I've got to warn you that Zeke can be a pain sometimes, so it's best that you put him in the paddock before starting to muck it out. Otherwise, he'll pester you incessantly for treats."

"I thought his name was Something Unexpected."

Sean nodded. "It is, officially. But when I first got him as a foal he didn't have a name. His baby coat was bay before it changed, and his mane shot up all over the place on his head and neck like a wild banshee, so I thought he looked like a Zeke. And before you ask why that name, I don't know. He's just always been that to me. Once you get to know him, you'll see it suits."

Shannon glanced behind her to the powerful gray stallion Sean was referring to, trying to picture him as a bay colt with a wild mane. It would have been hard to do if she hadn't grown up on a horse farm and witnessed firsthand how they could change coat colors as they matured. Sometimes it was nearly impossible to tell they were the same animal as adults. She imagined it was that way with Zeke, especially since he had no distinguishing white markings.

But boy, he must have been cute.

The horse's eyes were bright with curiosity and locked on her, his nostrils flaring as he caught her scent and waited patiently for her to stroll on over. "We'll be fine." Horses were one thing she knew how to handle.

"Lovely," Sean said and turned to go. He disappeared out the door and she leaned with a huge sigh against Zeke's stall door. She shut her eyes, thinking to take a moment and find her calm center.

That's when she heard, "Oh, and I'm flattered you like my body, Shannon. I'm fond of yours as well."

There went that plan all shot to hell.

Chapter Seven

SEAN ARRIVED BACK home and entered the stallion barn just in time to hear a commotion down at the far end. "Is everything all right?" he called out and moved quickly down the main aisle, peeking into each stall as he went.

A grunt came from Zeke's stall, then a thump and, "I said back, horse! You aren't getting these."

"Shite." He recognized Shannon's voice. "I'm coming!" Guaranteed Zeke was harassing her for oats, and Sean knew just how pushy he could be when he wanted something. He was worried the heavily muscled stallion might hurt her just by being a nuisance.

Arriving at the stall, he swung the door wide just in time to see his horse nudge Shannon with his nose, nickering and sniffing for treats in her pants. The Thoroughbred was so strong that the poor lass was flung backward and her flailing arm knocked the wheelbarrow full of fresh manure and straw over onto her as she hit the ground.

"Ah, Christ." He cringed and tried to wade into the stall to give her a hand up. The stench was pungent in its freshness and even though he was used to it, his eyes still watered. It was bad.

Shannon squealed and cursed and wiggled around trying to get out of the messy, smelly pile, only to have her boot slip, making her fall back into it. Sean shooed the stallion away and reached out a hand to her, which she promptly recoiled from, and she squeaked, "Don't touch me, I'm covered in horse shit!"

Despite himself, he smiled and laughed. The poor lass looked mortified. "I've seen worse," he said, though he actually hadn't. Still, her face looked like it was about to crumple and he didn't dare say something to cause it to fully collapse. He'd never been good with a woman's tears. They made him feel like an arse, and he would do anything he could to make them go away.

Saddest thing in the world was a beautiful woman crying.

She refused his hand a second time by shaking her head firmly. "No, thank you. I've got this," she ground out between clenched teeth and then started to get up again, this time making it all the way to her feet. Once in the clear, she looked at Sean, her face completely impassive and said in a modulated tone, "If you'll excuse me." And then she walked stiffly past him and out the barn, a large portion of her clothing covered in the stinky mess.

He felt terrible. "Shannon!" he called out behind her, but not really expecting an answer. He spotted her through the open stall door out to the paddock and sa that she was marching past at a very fast clip. "Shannon!" he called again before darting out of the barn after her. By the time he'd caught up to her, she'd reached the tree line at the edge of the river and then disappeared into the stand of aspens and grass.

"I wouldn't recommend jumping into the river if I were you. It'll be arse cold," Sean said only slightly joking, pretty certain she wouldn't but thinking he might want to throw it out there anyway just in case.

But it was too late. By the time he broke through the trees and reached the bank, Shannon had stripped down to a pale pink bra and knickers. Heat pooled in his groin and he came to instant, painful alert at the sight of her beautiful, curvy body nearly naked and on full display.

Try as he did, he couldn't get his mouth to make any sound. It had gone dry as vermouth the moment he'd glimpsed her. Which was really too bad because right then she leapt from the bank and splashed feet first into the frigid Rocky Mountain river. Her scream of anguish when she surfaced brought him to his senses and he rushed to the edge of the bank, his heart pumping.

"Are you crazy, woman?" he half-shouted as he began stripping off his favorite old shirt. "Get your arse out now before you catch cold."

Shannon dunked under water and resurfaced, stammering through chattering teeth as she moved back toward shore, "I had to do it, Muldoon. The stuff was in my hair."

Irritation rose in him, irrational and unwarranted. But damned if her jumping into the freezing fecking river hadn't upset him. Careless lass. "We've showers in the toilet for that purpose, you know." He growled.

Then she stood up in the river, the water rushing past at her waist, her cotton bra and knickers clinging transparently to her skin, and Sean's brain went on strike as all the remaining blood in his body went straight to his already stiff cock. Now his balls began to ache too as he couldn't help himself and raked his gaze hungrily over her body, soaking up the sensational sight.

Shannon was like a siren, her wet hair glimmering copper under the midday summer sun, her glorious body soft and curvy in all the right places. Her rounded hips and her small, trim waist had him almost ready to toss his deeply held convictions for just one taste of her.

Then he noticed the blue-purple tint of her lips and the spell was broken. Broken, but not gone. It'd be a very long time before he'd forget the sight of Shannon standing in the middle of the river like the Lady of the Lake.

Only he wasn't Arthur, and she could catch the death of her if she didn't get out immediately. He finished yanking his shirt off and thrust it out toward her. "Here, take this and put it on."

By the time she reached shore and took the shirt from his outstretched hand, she was visibly trembling and didn't argue, only said, "Thank you," and quickly slipped it on. And that's when a funny feeling overcame him at the sight of her in his faded, worn-out shirt as she worked it like a tent and removed her wet bra underneath. It was a feeling of rightness that wasn't entirely unwelcome—but it was pointless.

Because that thought frustrated him and he was still recovering from the shock of her jumping right into an icy river, Sean began searching for her soiled clothes and scooped them up by their edges. It was either that or he was going to snatch her up in a kiss that would leave them both stupid and breathless. And as great as that sounded at the moment, he knew in his heart it would be a terrible idea to follow through on.

It didn't mean he was ready to let her go yet, though. "You need to wash these clothes and the flat you're in doesn't have a machine. I'll fix that, but for now you'll have to use mine. Come with me now and I'll get them cleaning while you change into other clothes."

Shannon smiled gently as she walked past him, and he couldn't help noticing the way her nipples puckered against the thin worn fabric of his shirt. It was killing him—this was the second time that day she'd been bra-less in front of him.

"My only other change of clothes is dirty," she said as she found her boots by a nearby tree and gingerly picked them up. He noticed they were the tall English style ones.

"You can borrow mine," he replied automatically and began moving back through the trees toward his house. Shannon followed closely and they made their way across the property. It was only a few minutes before they were standing on the front porch of his house and even fewer before they were inside and he was filling the washing machine with laundry detergent.

Sean left the laundry room and found Shannon looking unhappy in the foyer. "What's wrong?" he asked, instantly worried that she didn't like his place and then pissed at himself for caring so much to begin with.

Her small pert nose was wrinkled and her expression uncertain when she asked him, "Do you mind if I shower while I wait for my clothes? I still feel pretty gross."

She might feel gross, but she looked wonderful to him—especially in his T-shirt. Why that was such a turn-on, he had no idea. "Of course," he replied and quickly grabbed her a change of clothes from his room. "Down the hall and to the right. Towels are in the cupboard." She might look like heaven, but the smell could definitely be better.

Knowing he needed to go before he did something dumb, Sean went and put on another T-shirt, then headed into his kitchen, where he started a pot of water to wet some tea and mentally talk down his hard-on. He spent the time he had to wait for the kettle to heat try-ing to think of anything other than Shannon wet and naked in his shower. Turned out it wasn't an easy thing to do, but he finally managed to get his thoughts and body under control through sheer force of will. Something about Shannon made both tasks much harder than he was used to.

The pot of tea had just finished steeping when she entered the kitchen, looking better than she had any right to in his pair of navy blue sweatpants and a light gray hoodie that was big and baggy on her—and some-thing lodged in his chest. Coughing in response to the increased pressure, Sean busied himself with pouring the tea into two mismatched ceramic mugs. He gave

Shannon the citrus orange one and brought the brown-flecked stoneware mug to his lips, taking a cautious sip. He liked his tea just this side of scalding.

Perfect.

"I like your house," she said after she took the offered mug from him and drank slowly. "Mmm, and thank you for the clothes and tea."

Sean glanced down at her beautiful face with its smattering of freckles and asked the question that had been on his mind. "Why do you only have one change of clothes, Shannon?" Was she running from something?

Her brown eyes shuttered and she shifted her gaze away, avoiding his when she answered, "Because I travel light."

His eyes narrowed. "Is that so? No transportation, no personal effects?"

He kept an eagle eye on her as she took another sip, looking oh so casual. "Nope. No need."

Something about this didn't seem right, but he couldn't put his finger on exactly what it was, so he changed the subject, knowing that if she were hiding something it would come out sooner or later. Didn't mean he couldn't prompt it to be sooner though. "Tell me about yourself." Sean took a good long sip of his tea and leaned back against the old farmhouse's outdated oak cupboards in the large eat-in kitchen.

She seemed to think about it for a minute before saying, "Before I showed up here, I was a professional equestrian."

That surprised him. "No shite?" He'd never have guessed it by the way she'd gotten so upset about the manure. Then again he had to admit that if it had been him covered in fresh horse crap, he'd have gotten upset too.

She nodded, her big brown eyes earnest. "It's true."

He took a moment to study her in the afternoon glow flooding in from the kitchen's big south-facing window over the sink and decided to believe her. What reason would she have to lie?

"Okay, I believe you. Why did you quit?"

"My overall performance was less than stellar." She looked uncomfortable and sad for a moment.

Because she suddenly looked lonely, he said, "Have you asked yourself why that was?"

Seeming to look at a point over his shoulder, he saw her brown eyes darken with some emotion. "Because it's never what I really wanted to do with my life to begin with, but I did it to please my parents."

"I joined the school rugby team when I was fifteen to make me mum happy." He could still recall the surprise on her face when he told her. "Made me a miserable feck and I quit the next week. Doing things to try and make parents happy always ends badly."

"Amen," she agreed over the rim of her mug. When their gazes locked, she held his and said, "What about you? What were you doing before you came over here to America?"

Looking into her beautiful eyes filled with such innocent curiosity, Sean found himself sharing the truth. "I was a bare-knuckle boxer back in Dublin."

Her delicately arched eyebrows shot up. "Get out, no way!"

"God's truth. I've been boxing since I was barely more than a kid." He couldn't help smiling over her incredulous tone.

She blinked at him, her eyes big and round. "That's bad ass. Why'd you quit then?"

Finding it easy to share with Shannon, he crossed his long, muscular legs and thought about how best to answer. "Because I got in over my head with my manager on a business deal I wasn't equipped to handle. And then I was involved in a very unfortunate betting circuit that went arseways."

"That sucks."

The matter-of-fact way she said it made him laugh. "Aye, it did. But it was a long time ago. I got my horse out of the deal and a fresh start. I'm happy now."

"How long have you been in horseracing?"

Sean scratched his stubbly chin and thought about it for a minute. "About three years, give or take. Before that I worked on a horse ranch in the next valley over and learned my way around the business."

The way she tipped her head to the side and chewed her bottom lip as she gazed at him with such interest was slowly driving him insane. It was the most innocent seduction, made all the more arousing by her complete and utter lack of awareness around it.

Thankfully, just when he thought he couldn't take it anymore, she quit working that plump bottom lip and asked, "So how did you end up with this place?"

Grinning wide because it was still damn funny to him, Sean said with his accent exaggerated, "I found me pot of gold at the end of the rainbow." She laughed appreciatively even as she eyed him quizzically. He continued to explain, feeling oddly proud that he'd made her smile like that, "About nine months after I moved to Fortune, my mates Jake and Aidan and I got wrecked off some of Jake's homemade ale and went panning for gold in the creek behind his cabin. And we literally struck gold."

"Are you kidding?" she exclaimed.

He shook his head. "Totally serious. The three of us made out like thieves with those gold nuggets when we cashed in. So I bought this horse ranch, Jake opened a brewpub in town called Two Moons, and Aidan expanded his business."

"That's unbelievable," she said, looking a little dazed as she shook her head at him. It was a far out story, he knew.

"The locals have called the three of us the Bachelors of Fortune ever since." He rubbed the back of his neck and added, "It's meant to be a term of endearment."

She laughed at that. "Oh, I just bet it is."

Moving next to him, Shannon began rinsing her empty mug in the sink. As she scrubbed, she kept stealing shy glances at him out of the corner of her eyes, starting at his feet and working her way up. He had to bite back a laugh when she came to his waist and bobbled the mug, almost dropping it in the sink. When her gaze finally met his, she blushed deeply and broke eye contact, but her lips curved in a small, sweet smile. He could smell the scent of his soap on her, she was so close, and it made his gut tighten with rekindled desire—and some other emotion he refused to name because he *liked* her smelling like him. It made him feel possessive and territorial and protective.

Riding on the feeling, Sean reached out a hand and brushed a strand of damp hair behind her ear, his fingertips caressing the delicate skin of her neck with the movement. "You have the most beautiful hair," he said softly, almost reverently. His senses were captivated by her warmth and beauty.

Lost to her and the moment, Sean lowered his head until his lips grazed the freckles on her cheekbone. The way she trembled under his touch and inhaled softly, her lips parting gently, lit a fire of need inside him. Unable to stop, he captured her lips with his and groaned at the heat of contact.

Like a match to a tinderbox, he went up in flames. On a growl he wrapped her up in his arms and pulled her close, glorying in the feel of her lush body pressed hard against him. Running his hands over her back until they fisted in her still damp hair, Sean took the kiss deep, and nearly came undone when Shannon opened eagerly for him on a sexy moan, and their tongues brushed in a passionate mating that made him burn brighter than he ever had before. With his cock straining hard and aching against the fly of his jeans, he pushed into her and reveled in the way her body cradled him in response. The heat coming from between her thighs nearly buckled his knees.

He didn't want it to end. He wanted more.

Taking it, Sean released her hair and found the edge of her sweatshirt with his fingertips. Lifting the fabric, he skimmed his palms up her ribcage and smiled against her lips when his fingers brushed the bottom curve of her breasts and she let out a breathy sound, arching into his hands.

Needing even more, he found her puckered nipples and pinched gently, fueled on by her husky gasp of pleasure. "You like that, don't you?" he whispered against her lips, desire making his movements more urgent now. He pinched them again and rolled them between his fingers until she dropped her head back and her eyes drifted closed, a small feline smile of pleasure on her lips.

Instead of answering, she moved a hand down his body, caressing gently until she reached his throbbing hard-on and squeezed him through his jeans. Exquisite, torturous pleasure tore through him, and lust so strong it nearly overwhelmed him reared up and knocked him for a loop. His body jerked and went rigid from the shock of the intensity of emotion.

Shannon must have felt it or sensed it or something because she yanked away and blushed profusely. "I'm sorry. I shouldn't have done that. I should be going."

Still reeling from what he'd just experienced, Sean was slow to respond and didn't find his voice until she'd collected her clothes from the dryer and was already gone. Blowing out a slow breath, he raked a hand through his hair and tried to make sense of what had just happened, but his brain was simply too flooded by hormones to function properly, and he gave up. Some things a guy just had to suck up and accept, as much as it pained him.

Sean let the truth settle as he watched her rush barefoot down the drive carrying her small bundle of clothes, and he inwardly flinched at the implications. The proof was in the pudding.

Shannon was his kryptonite.

Chapter Eight

"How is a woman supposed to get any snooping done around here when there's no one around to ask questions of?" Shannon grumbled early the next afternoon.

That morning Sean; his team of men; and his champion Thoroughbred, Something Unexpected, aka Zeke—along with several other stakes racers—had left for Long Island, New York, where they would run in the final installments of the Triple Crown trifecta in the Belmont Stakes this upcoming Saturday. A few stable hands had been left behind to care for the remaining horses, but they were deceptively wily. She'd yet to corner one for a conversation. In fact, she hadn't seen one all day, but from the fresh stall bedding for the mares and foals, she knew they were around.

At first she'd thought everyone being gone would be the perfect opportunity to go rifling through things for information or evidence, but she'd been wrong. Three hours of painstakingly reviewing the accounting books and online files had turned up absolutely nothing and only proven to be a lesson in tedium. The large gray metal medicine cabinet where vaccines and needles and such were stored was locked. Solid. She'd tried jimmying it but couldn't get it to budge. One of the stable hands had to have the key, but she wasn't in the mood to wait all day for one to finally show up. Still, she made a mental note to check the locker for steroids the first chance she got.

Next she'd thought about Sean's faded yellow farmhouse. It was sitting there, ripe for the picking—or snooping, rather. So she'd left the stables and jogged up the gravel lane until the traditional two-story home came into view. Appreciating the ambiance it exuded, tucked as it was behind a thick stand of aspens and shaded by two enormous oak trees, Shannon crossed the large flat lawn and climbed the front porch.

That's when she discovered the front door was locked. And the back one. And all the windows she could safely reach.

Though she was disappointed, Shannon accepted that the day was a bust on Sean's place, but that maybe there was something else she could try so she wouldn't sit around biting her nails and getting all worked up and worried. Earlier while canvassing the property, she'd noticed an older generation Ford work truck with the keys left in the ignition. Because she knew that was a quirk of farm vehicles—the keys rarely left them—she wasn't worried that she was accidently absconding with somebody's personal truck. Especially since a faded, mostly peeled Pine Creek Ranch logo was still visible on the driver side door.

Besides, Sean wouldn't want her stuck out in the boonies all by herself, would he? He didn't know it, but he'd want her to drive into town and try to hit up the locals, see if they had anything juicy to share about him. Oh no, wait. That's what *she* wanted.

She should have asked him in person, but the flood of embarrassment that had filled her unexpectedly the moment she'd spotted him drinking from his stoneware mug on the front porch that morning, looking tough and rugged and sinfully sexy in a snug black T-shirt, worn jeans, and his wool cap, had had her tucking tail and deciding that she'd figure out the answer on her own. Better that than have to talk to the man she'd groped shamelessly the day before.

What the hell had she been thinking?

That was the question that played in her mind the whole windy, seven-mile drive into town. What had possibly possessed her to make out with Sean in the first place? Didn't she care about her family? And did she not care that he might be a seriously unethical man?

The only answer that she could come up with sounded so Jerry Maguire—*You complete me*—and kind of cheesy that she didn't want to admit the truth even to herself. Not even alone in a soundproof dark room. It was *so* bad. So she shoved it aside with pretty much everything else she was in denial about at the moment—which was about 99 percent of everything in her life.

It hadn't been an especially good few months.

Shannon found a parking spot on Main Street and paralleled it, pulling the F150 to a stop under the shady canopy of a honey locust tree and setting the e-brake. It was a quirk of hers that she always pulled the e-brake no matter if the place she'd parked warranted the extra help or not. When she climbed out, she was instantly taken with the lively, happy energy of the town. People in casual outdoor clothing with labels from companies such as The North Face, Marmot, REI, and the like strolled leisurely down the sidewalk next to thrift shop hippies and true-blue cowboys, their suntans and windswept hair giving testament to their united love affair with Colorado's great outdoors—and many of them walking dogs, which she was beginning to suspect should be the state's official animal because they were *everywhere*.

She loved dogs and wanted one someday, but she swore that the relationship between dog and man in Colorado was on a whole other level—almost symbiotic mutualism like those birds that caravanned around on the backs of rhinos in Africa, depending upon each other for survival and protection.

Even now, a woman in yoga pants passed with her dog and a double wide jogging stroller containing two hefty-sized toddlers. Shannon scrunched her nose in confusion and more than a little admiration. How did she do that? Wouldn't one of those accessories be hard enough to handle on their own?

Shaking her head, Shannon pocketed her keys, thankful that her clothes were clean and stench-free once again. Meeting the town's residents for the first time while smelling like something a dog had just eaten and then regurgitated wasn't exactly how she'd planned for it to go. She was nervous enough to begin with. Meeting new people always made her uncomfortable.

The Old West-style wood-front buildings were painted in daring, bold colors—like lime green, fuchsia, and violet kind of bold. Shannon had just stopped to admire the window display in one when her phone rang. Pulling it from the small quilted purse she'd stored in her duffle while traveling, she thumbed open the touch screen and read the caller ID, instantly frowning.

There went her mood.

Sucking in a deep breath, Shannon pasted a big, bright smile on her face. "Hi, Dad!" she said in a completely forced, cheerful voice. Really what she wanted to do was hurtle the smartphone as far into space as she could and hope that it never came back. The town tugged at her and she wished for a second that she was just a normal, average tourist visiting and not there to lie and sneak.

"What's the status?" Callum Charlemagne said, cutting to the chase, no affection remotely perceivable in his voice.

Because her chest suddenly felt two sizes too tight and her pulse was scrambling, Shannon swallowed hard and replied carefully, "I haven't been able to find anything yet."

She swore she just heard her father growl. Like an animal. She'd never heard him make such an undignified sound in her life. "Shannon, let me make something clear. This Irishman, this *Sean Muldoon*, came out of nowhere three years ago—no background, no history of connection to the sport. Practically overnight his horses have swept all the major stakes, stealing the Triple Crown right out from under our very own Rocket Man—the fastest racer we've had for decades! And now everybody wants their mares bred to his stakes winners. They've abandoned tradition and history in favor of this gigolo's breeding program. This family has been invested in racing for generations and now we're on the verge of collapse. We are out of money, nearly impoverished. It's all because of him. Find. Me. Something." He paused and then added much more quietly, "Before it's too late. You're the only one who can do this. We're counting on you."

"Maybe you should have hired a professional," Shannon said, her voice unsteady.

"With what money, Shannon?" he demanded to know. "That bastard has taken almost everything. It's all on you."

Tears stung Shannon's eyes and she blinked hard, struggling for composure. Way to bring the guilt *and* the hammer of gloom and doom. "I'm doing my best, Dad."

"Try harder," he rebuffed harshly. "I don't think you sufficiently grasp what's at stake."

Feeling the slap like it was physical, her anxiety spiked and she began to shake. Insecurity slammed into her hard and she clamped down viciously, refusing to let it gain control of her thoughts. But it didn't stop her breath from coming in fast bursts and her heart from pounding.

She closed her eyes and tried to focus around the feelings. She would ignore his comment and not legitimize it by responding. "I had a conversation with him last night and he shared quite a bit about himself. I'm not sure this guy is corrupt like you think he is, Dad." She thought back to the rags-to-riches tale he'd shared last night. "He might just be incredibly lucky."

"Don't be silly," he scolded, sounding irritated. "There's no such thing."

Though she wanted to argue, Shannon recognized the futility of it as well as the time that would be wasted and decided to let it go. Yet she couldn't resist pushing just a little more before she did. Watching a woman who looked remarkably like a salt-and-pepper pixied Jamie Lee Curtis open the fire-engine-red door to the Fortune Food Co-op, she made a mental note to check that place out first and said, "The guy grew up on the streets in Dublin, Dad. He had it pretty bad I assume, because he mentioned being a boxer as a kid to help his mom pay the rent."

The line went dead silent.

One heartbeat.

Two.

Finally a tight, clipped, "He boxed, you say?"

Not registering the edgy, excited tone because she was too relieved that he hadn't barked back at her and shut her down, she offered freely, "Yeah, he said it was bare-knuckle, if that means anything." She was pretty sure it meant fighting without gloves, but she had less than no knowledge about boxing and didn't really plan to gain any, honestly. It just seemed brutish and unnecessary. But with how he'd explained things, she understood why

Sean had and didn't hold it against him. "And apparently he was pretty good. Right up until he got tangled up in a bet with some bad people and his career ended over it."

Her father cleared his throat. "Well, I see. This information is very helpful."

And that was the best she was going to get from him, as far as compliments or positive reinforcement went. Because she was still working to control her worries, she accepted it for what it was and decided to put her energies to better use. "I'm glad," she said, though she wasn't sure what Sean's days as a boxer had to do with horseracing.

"I'm leaving for Belmont in the morning. I have to go," boomed her father unexpectedly, the sound coming briskly through the receiver, and then Shannon was left with nothing but dead air as the call disconnected. More than a little disconcerted at the abruptness with which the talk had ended, she glanced around to regain her bearings and took long, slow, deep breaths in an attempt to settle her heart rate back to normal.

It really was a beautiful town, she thought as she took in the looming snow-capped peak above her that was part of the mountain range bending in a U-shape around Fortune. Enormous planters were set up and down the sidewalk and overflowed with healthy, lush, multicolored flowers and decorative grasses. Some of the storefronts had old-fashioned wooden signs hung suspended over their doors from metal poles. Others, like the food co-op, had huge painted signs plastered to the front of them, declaring their names with artistic flair.

What would it be like to live here?

The thought captivated her as she spotted the Old West saloon-style Two Moons Brewery and Pub across the street. The rustic building, with the huge, open brick patio, sat on the corner of Main and a side street; she could just make out from the distance that it was named Timberline. It was next to a snazzy retail cycling and repair shop that had a retro-fabulous vintage poster in the front window of legendary road cyclist Eddy Merckx capturing the gold during the 1970 Tour de France. And next to that business was a clapboard-front, old-fashioned donut bakery called Hole in The Wall that sported a scalloped awning over the front-window display of donut delights in varying glazes, shapes, and fillings. It all proved too delicious-looking to resist.

Nodding pleasantly to a couple of elderly ladies with thin, colored poofs of hair and polyester pants as they passed in front of her, Shannon went to the crosswalk like a good citizen and quickly crossed the street. There was no way she was passing up a chance to have a freshly baked bear claw.

She was just passing the plain wood bench that sat in front of the brewpub that Sean had mentioned his friend owned when the double saloon doors swung open and a young, blond-haired woman exited, frowning fiercely.

When she spotted Shannon, she threw up her hands and declared, "That man is *such* a jerk!" Her enviable cleavage rose as she breathed heavily, clearly unhappy with someone. The way her blue eyes flashed behind her oversized reading glasses made Shannon feel almost sorry for the guy who'd ticked her off.

"Guys," Shannon said wryly, immediately sympathetic and feeling the sisterly bond, the one that connected all women around the world through the singular, universal understanding that men were inevitably going to piss them off. They couldn't help it. Globally, women understood this genetic defect in their counterparts and loved them still in spite of it. Maybe because of it—who knew? Men kept things spicy, that was for sure.

The instant she thought it, last night's escapade with Sean flashed through her head like a movie on the big screen—him all hard and manly and unbelievably scrumptious, and her all slutty and low-class like high school's easy-queen, Sara Merger. One part of her was all, *"Dammmn, girl,"* and impressed with herself. The other part—the part of her that used to be *all* of her until she'd met the gorgeous Irishman—was down-to-her-bones embarrassed at her behavior. Acting like a college sorority girl after too many shots wasn't like her. She had never been physical with a guy that she wasn't in a relationship with. So this new *Girls Gone Wild* side of her was jarring and worrisome. More so was the fact that Muldoon had brought it out in her to begin with.

Immersed in her thoughts, she was taken off guard when the gladiator-sandal-wearing blond grabbed her arm, tucked it through hers like they were lifelong best friends, and began walking. Shannon fell into step with her as she said, "You'd think by now that I would know better than to ask him nicely for anything." She shook her head vigorously enough to loosen her bun. "But *nooo*," she drawled. "I just keep on being Little Miss Polite and patient like a fool, making it far too easy for him to not take me seriously and blow me off."

"Umm," Shannon began, not having even the foggiest idea what the gal was talking about. It wasn't clear whether she really wanted a response anyway.

Her new acquaintance heaved a great big sigh and laid her head on Shannon's shoulder before asking softly, "What am I going to do?"

Sympathy filled her at the weary undertone and inspiration struck. Stopping abruptly, Shannon stated matter-of-factly, "You're going to stop asking him nicely, that's what you're going to do."

"I am?" her new friend asked and blinked, her eyes magnified and owllike behind the thick tortoise shell frames. In that moment she looked like a blond Zooey Deschenel from *New Girl*.

Convinced for reasons unknown, Shannon nodded. "Yes. If this guy isn't responding to nice, then try something different. Try assertive or coercive or mean. Oh! Or try naughty." What guy could ever resist that approach? Especially if it came with a rack like that?

"That's genius!" the blond said, perking up and coming to a stop in front of the donut bakery. The aroma was beyond amazing. Lifting her head from Shannon's shoulder, she introduced herself. "I'm Apple, by the way."

Already liking her, she replied, "Shannon."

Hitching a thumb over her shoulder back toward the brewpub, Apple said with no small amount of frustration in her tone, "And the jerk I'm currently mad at is Jake Stone, the no-good owner of Two Moons."

Looking back at the business, Shannon noticed a male figure in the window and asked, "Is he tall and muscular, with dark blond hair, face stubble, and a pretty intense frown?"

Apple closed her eyes and groaned. "He's still doing that? *Really?* That man has a perma-scowl, I swear."

Considering, Shannon sized him up and decided, "He's still hot."

Her friend sighed. "Yeah, he is."

Hot or not, he was Sean's friend and she wanted to talk to him, pick his brain to see what he knew. But before she could, Apple latched onto her arm again and said as she resumed walking, leading Shannon farther off track, "Change of subject. Since I've never seen you before and I've lived here my whole life, I'm assuming you're either visiting or have just moved here."

Neither, actually, but it wasn't something she could really share. She was supposed to be incognito. "Just moved. I'm the new stable manager out at Pine Creek Ranch."

Apple's pretty face lit up. "You're working for Sean Muldoon? Oh, I adore him! He's a regular at the library and comes in every Saturday to check out exactly two books. And last winter when Mr. Concannon had to cancel on us at the last minute because his gout flared up real bad, Sean pitched in and played his fiddle, saving the kids' concert with his Irish folk songs. I'll never forget the way he made those children laugh with some of his G-rated limericks."

So the guy was a book lover and helped out the community when he could? Now *that* was some seriously suspect behavior. Better leap on that one fast before he went and did something really criminal like save a puppy from a burning building.

Torn between questioning Jake and finding out everything her friend knew, Shannon had the choice taken out of her hands when Apple opened the door to the bright and airy food co-op with handmade quilts decorating the walls and announced loudly, "Hey everyone, we have a new resident in town! She's just started working out at Pine Creek Ranch. Introduce yourselves and help Shannon feel welcome."

Any determination to follow her father's orders evaporated in a puff of smoke when about a half-dozen people looked up from what they were doing and said hello almost in unison. Half-convinced she'd entered the Twilight Zone, Shannon said hello back, but her feelings must have shown on her face because Apple looked at her with concern and said, "Are you okay?" Then her hand flew to her breast like she had a shocking revelation. "Oh my God, was that weird?"

Umm…only *completely*.

Apple rushed on, "It's just, I volunteer here and know everyone." She rapped her head with her knuckles gently. "I didn't think. I'm so sorry if I embarrassed you."

"It's okay," she assured her new friend, even though she now felt like about a million eyes were on her, watching her every movement. And that was exactly the last thing she needed when she was supposed to be snooping.

Dear old Dad was not going to be pleased.

With a sinking feeling in her gut, Shannon was about to call the entire day a bust when the Jamie Lee Curtis lookalike from earlier approached her with a friendly, open smile. "Hi, I'm June." Then she leaned in and whispered conspiratorially, "Tell me, what's it like working for that hunky Irishman?"

She laughed self-consciously before realizing that the entire store had heard the woman's question and gone dead quiet waiting for her answer. A quick glance around confirmed at least three pair of female eyes were looking at her expectantly. Apparently she wasn't the only one in town to think Sean made quite an impression.

"It's, umm," she began, tucking her hands awkwardly into her front pockets and fumbling to say to her mini-audience, "nice?"

It was like a dam had burst, because half a dozen women rushed her and all began speaking at once. She was bombarded with comments and questions about the Bachelor of Fortune. Apparently they couldn't wait to gossip about the "available hottie," as one woman put it.

As the women swarmed her, Shannon took a deep, bracing breath and realized that this was exactly what she'd been hoping for: townspeople willing to tell her about Sean. Seizing the opportunity, she plastered on a grin, and dove headfirst into the gossip-fest.

Gushing over Sean with a bunch of women was business. Yeah, business. It had nothing to do with her wanting to know for personal reasons. And butterflies hadn't launched into flight in the pit of her belly at the mere thought of him.

Nope. Not at all. She had no feelings about him one way or the other.

Her heart skipped a beat. *Shit*. She was in trouble. This had never happened to her before.

She couldn't even lie to herself.

Chapter Nine

"COME QUICK, MR. MULDOON! Zeke's been injured!"

Sean looked up from his Belmont Stakes catalog in
alarm. "Come again?" he said to his assistant trainer,
Tracy Webb, hoping he hadn't heard the guy right. His
horse had been the picture of health when he'd checked
on him an hour ago.

The young horseman's face was grave. "I'm sorry, sir,
but it just happened. The vet is with him now. I'm not
sure the extent of the damage, but it looks bad. You better
come real quick."

Lunging out of his seat, Sean dropped the catalog and
began running across the expansive park in a full-out
sprint. He didn't stop until he'd reached the stall where
the Triple Crown champion was being boarded. A small
crowd of onlookers was milling around, as well as a local
news camera crew that must have already caught wind
of his horse's injury. He flung out his arms like he was

shooing away a bunch of hungry pigeons, fear and worry for his horse making him gruff as he none too gently waded his way through to Zeke. "Off with all of you!"

The crowd parted for him with a grumble, and Sean reached the gate, fear gripping him and making it hard to remain clearheaded.

One of Belmont's resident veterinarians was crouched down next to his beloved Zeke, the horse prone and obviously sedated. Sean refused to consider that he wasn't moving for another reason. "What happened?" he croaked around the hard lump in his throat and wanted to go to his side, but found his foot rooted to the spot. "How is he?"

The vet replied, her gaze filled with kindness and sympathy, "He'll live, Mr. Muldoon, but he got a nasty gash that severed an artery and a major tendon. He's lost a lot of blood."

Pressing his lips together to stem their trembling, Sean looked at the fresh bandage wrapped around the gray's lower hindquarter. "Thank you, doctor, for the help. Do you have any idea what made the wound?" *What the bleedin' hell could've caused that kind of harm?*

His stable hand Joe spoke up. "I found this in the stall when I first discovered him. You'll want to take a look."

The young Texan held up a long, skinny, jagged splinter of wood. The tip was covered in blood. It looked like it was a broken-off piece of something bigger—like possibly the handle of a pitchfork.

Unease crept down Sean's spine and he whipped up his head, surveying the small crowd that still lingered in the corridor. There was no reason for anything like that splinter to have been in the stall in the first place because all of his team was studious in picking up after themselves. And that meant that if something had been left in the stall big enough to seriously injure Zeke, it certainly hadn't been left there by his men.

Someone else had to have been in the stall. Recently too—within the past hour, when his team had been on break and the stallion was left unattended. And that meant that this was no accident.

It was bloody fecking upsetting.

Finally uprooted, Sean moved to crouch down next to the Thoroughbred, anger beginning to brew in his gut. He stroked the stallion's silky coat, struggling not to see red when someone said from behind him, "Well, now, isn't this a sad sight?"

Sean whipped his head around and scowled when he saw the arsehole. "Mr. Charlemagne." It didn't matter one bit to him that his visitor was from the oldest founding family in the racing business and was considered by most to be an industry legend, or that the horses his farm produced were a nearly constant stream of stakes winners. The guy was still an arsehole.

Callum Charlemagne smiled at him tightly, although with the way his lip curled it looked a lot more like a snarl. "Muldoon," he begrudgingly said, rude as always. He'd never much liked Sean as far as he could tell, not since he'd come out of nowhere with Something Unexpected and started giving Charlemagne some real competition.

They eyed each other in tense silence while the vet packed up her things. When she left with a promise to check back on Zeke in an hour, Sean was stuck alone with the pompous, egocentric man.

Sean gave his horse one last pat and rose to his feet. "Is there something I can do for you?" He wanted the bastard gone so he could get on with finding out who did this to Zeke.

"Not at all. You've already done more than enough."

The way the weasel said it had Sean clenching a fist, the urge to punch him in the nose almost overwhelming. But since he hadn't thrown even a single blow since he'd left Ireland, he wasn't going to lose control and backslide now. He'd left that part of himself there as surely as he'd left his God-given surname.

Charlemagne leaned his elbows on the stall gate and added, "That injury is a real shame. Your horse will be lucky to walk again without a limp. His racing days are most definitely over." He finished with a *tsk-tsk* and a shake of his head like he actually cared.

Anger bubbled up hard and fast inside, and Sean rounded, his hands clenched into fists. The pisser wasn't even trying to hide his glee. "Have a care with what you say, Mr. Charlemagne. You wouldn't be wanting it taken out of context and discover yourself a suspect with the police if this proves not to be an accident, now would you?"

It wasn't even worth the effort to disguise the threat. Someone was after Sean, and though deep down he was worried that Mickey O'Banion and his men had finally uncovered him, he wanted it well-known and widespread that he wasn't hesitating to share this information with the local authorities on the chance that this was a simple straightforward case of jealousy and sabotage, and the perpetrator was someone from the racing circuit.

"Is that a threat, son?" Charlemagne narrowed his beady eyes and slowly straightened.

Unfazed, Sean met his hard stare with one of his own. "Only if there's a reason for it to be."

"Oh, you've plenty of reasons," he scoffed.

"So, you did this to me horse then?" If that bastard were responsible for the attack on Zeke, then he would live to regret it. Sean would make sure of it.

The industry heavyweight must have realized his position and held up his hands in a display of innocence, his furrowed brow melting into a practiced smile. "Not me, Muldoon." He took a step in retreat and added, "You let me know if I can be of help though, you hear? I'd be happy to provide a statement to the police, if need be." He made that *tsk-tsk* sound again and shook his head. "Really is a shame."

My, how a tune can change in an instant, Sean thought cynically. "That's kind of you to say."

Clearly not well acquainted with the concept of sarcasm, Charlemagne nodded regally as if Sean had paid him an actual compliment. "I do what I can."

Just then a blur of movement caught his eye and Sean jerked. *What the bloody hell*? He dashed out of the stall, his heart suddenly pounding furiously.

"Excuse me," he said belatedly to Charlemagne, already making his way down the long corridor, his gaze scanning the crowd for another glimpse of the person he'd thought he'd seen—the same person whose reflection had been in the window at Jake's brewery.

Billy Hennessey.

"Stay with Zeke, Joe," he called out. If it was Billy, somebody needed to watch over the stallion's safety.

Forgetting instantly about his bickering with the old horse breeder, Sean navigated his way around a couple riders who were leading their horses out for some exercise, and he broke into a run when he caught sight of the person in the plain black hoodie disappearing around the south end of the stables and slipping outside.

"Hey!" Sean shouted, the blood draining from his face.

He wanted desperately to deny it, but the way the person in the sweatshirt moved seemed so familiar to him. He knew someone who moved like that, someone bad.

"Hey!" Sean called again, refusing to give in to the fear that it was indeed the hired gun. Lots of people held one shoulder higher than the other. It could be anyone. He had no reason to believe that he'd been discovered.

But then why had Zeke been hurt?

If it were someone threatened by his rising success in the business, the attacker would have taken down his three-year-old Triple Crown contender, Colorado Gold. That made more sense than to go after the previously crowned champion.

Reaching the end of the stables and rounding the corner, Sean caught sight of the person in the black hoodie just as he dashed between two outbuildings. With rising alarm and anger, he charged after. Breathing hard when he burst out the other side of the two buildings, Sean scanned left and right, but saw nothing.

The hood had disappeared.

"Shite!" He swore. Man, what was wrong with him? Chasing random people around simply because he had a growing sense of dread hanging over his head? Feck, maybe he needed to see a shrink. Because the fact of the matter was that he had no hard evidence that Mickey O'Banion and his men had anything to do with Zeke's injury. He hadn't exactly endeared himself to the racing community. They embraced tradition and he simply didn't fit their ideal. Still, it had never caused him concern before.

Then again, he'd never had a horse come up suspiciously lame before a race like Zeke had, either.

Raking a hand through his hair, Sean swore again, feeling anxious and jittery to get back to Zeke. Maybe he was just losing his mind. Though he'd built a life that pleased him, he'd never stopped looking over his shoulder, and it was wearing him down.

An image of Shannon flashed in his mind and he sighed, this time for a whole different reason. That woman made him want things. Things that came with commitments and attachments—neither of which he was in any place to accept. Still, it didn't stop him from wondering what it might be like to have a warm, soft woman to come home to after a shite day like this. He turned around and began making his way back to the stable, eager to be with his horse.

If that woman were Shannon, it wouldn't be a hardship.

Grinning at the delightful thought of climbing into bed next to her soft, sleep-warmed body, Sean didn't see it coming until it was too late. Until a sharp, searing pain erupted in the back of his head.

And his world went black around him.

Chapter Ten

"WHEN I CAME to, I was lying with my face in the dirt and with a lump the size of a fecking watermelon on my head. But Zeke is back home and safe, thank God, and that's what really matters. I bloody hate that he's hurt, though. It still makes me mad," Sean said around the rim of a pint glass to Jake two days later as his mate pulled microbrews from a tap and listened to his tale like a good bartender, interjecting with a comment or question here and there.

"Understandable. And there weren't any witnesses who saw what happened?" Aidan asked as he dumped an unholy amount of hot sauce onto a basket of seasoned chips. It was all Sean could do not to cringe when he shoved a bunch in his mouth and started chewing. He'd grown up on Irish food—it wasn't known for its spice. The smell wafting off the potatoes alone was enough to make his eyes water.

How did the guy eat like that on a regular basis and still have any taste buds left?

The jukebox in the far corner of the brewpub changed over and Taylor Swift came on, talking about what it felt like to be twenty-two. Glancing around at the dozen or so customers, Sean couldn't help noticing that Apple happened to be one of them. The librarian was sitting in a corner booth with a pint of beer and a plate stacked with chips and a juicy looking cheeseburger. Every so often she would look over at Jake and frown. Why he didn't just give the poor lass an hour of his time to answer a few questions was beyond him. It seemed like a simple enough request.

Then again, this was Jake. He was contrary just for the fun of it.

Aidan regained his attention. "Hey, did that hit to the head do some damage you need to have checked out? I've asked you a question three times."

Blinking, Sean apologized. "Sorry, mate. What was the question?" He couldn't remember. Huh. Maybe he did need to get checked out. Or maybe it was knowing that someone was out there trying to sabotage him that had him feeling out of sorts.

Yeah, maybe.

Aidan's hazel eyes filled with concern. "I asked if there were any witnesses to the attack."

Sean shook his head and flinched when it throbbed from the movement. "No, I asked around and nobody saw anything."

Just having finished filling a drink order, Jake wiped his hands on the towel he had tucked into his belt and crossed his arms. "And you didn't go to the cops?"

Involving the guards was the last thing he wanted to do. "No, I didn't." Jake's face went stormy and Sean continued quickly, "Look, I know what you're thinking, but there's no actual evidence that whoever attacked me had anything to do with what happened to Zeke." Still, his gut told him that they were connected. He just didn't want his friends to worry needlessly.

Besides, as close as he was to the two men, there were still many things about him they didn't know, his past entanglements being one of them. It wasn't a matter of trust. He had kept his real motivation for coming to America a secret from others for their own safety. The less they knew, the safer they were. And he intended to keep it that way.

Jake scowled hotly. "I still don't like it." He slapped a glass down suddenly on the bar with a sharp rap and exploded. "Damn it, man, when are you going to trust me and Aidan? When your past comes back to bite you and you wind up dead?"

The surprise he felt at Jake's perceptiveness must have shown on his face because his friend paced away angrily before coming back and leaning on the glossy wood bar with both elbows and pegging Sean with a hard look. "You didn't really think we were that stupid, did you?" Unclenching a hand, he straightened his index finger and flexed his wrist, pointing his finger back and forth between the two. "Hell, we've known you were hiding from something since they day you showed up in town with nothing to your name but a damn horse."

Aidan clapped him hard on the shoulder. "Truth, pal. Jake here called it from the get-go."

And all this bloody time he'd thought he'd been stealthy. Well, there went his comfortable illusion. "Be that as it may, it's best for you both if you keep your nose clean from me business." Outside of his mum, the two of them were the closest thing to family he'd ever had. He'd never forgive himself if something happened to them.

Jake scoffed openly. "You think that's going to scare us off?"

Recognizing the futility of it, Sean stared hard at the bit of ale still at the bottom of his pint before saying, "I know it won't, mate."

The pub owner nodded. "Damn straight."

That must have settled something because Aidan changed the subject. "Tell me more about this new stable manager of yours."

Instantly his mind turned to Shannon, and his mood lifted about thirty octaves and his chest went warm and fuzzy. Bloody great. Swell.

Now there was that to worry about too.

THAT SAME EVENING back at the ranch Shannon jimmied the lock on the back door of Sean's house with her credit card and cursed life's cruelty. Zeke had been injured at Belmont three days ago and was all bandaged up and grumpy now that he was home and recovering in his stall. It made her fuss over him like a sick baby and angry that he'd been hurt to begin with.

Sean had been evasive about how it had happened too, saying something dismissive about a broken pitchfork. It made her wonder if there was more to the story than he was sharing. Although, to be fair, he'd still been pretty upset when he'd relayed the event to her, so he might have just spaced on some details. Still, his lack of disclosure was a little frustrating—especially since she was quickly growing to love Zeke as much as he did.

And boy, her father had really put the screws to her this time. Threatening to withdraw all financial support from Colleen, leaving her hung out to dry when she was at such a critical point on her path to becoming a doctor, was a really, really low blow.

It was also damned effective.

She grunted in relief when the lock finally gave. Pocketing her card, she quickly slipped inside and closed the door behind her. Whatever she was looking for she needed to find fast. Earlier, she'd overheard him tell one of the stable hands that he was heading into town for a bit, and that had been almost two hours ago. Since she'd been ruthlessly going over his ledgers once again, trying to find any little discrepancy, she'd lost track of the time.

Finding that she was in Sean's kitchen, Shannon forced her shoulders to relax and took a moment to let it all sink in. The first time she'd been in his house she had been so freaked out by the poo in her hair that she couldn't have described what it looked like if she'd been paid to because nothing had registered. Taking things in now as she moved through his space felt like the first time.

And she very much liked what she saw. The big old farmhouse wasn't flashy, but it was sturdy and filled with the same denim blue furniture as her apartment above the stables. It had a comfortable, easy feel to it and tons of natural light. The oak floors were scarred and in need of refinishing but were still beautiful.

It had always been a secret dream of hers to live in a place like this. Some place that felt cozy and safe and welcoming. And where children would grow up in a family that was close knit and ate dinner together every night at the table in the country kitchen while a dog dozed on the rug in front of the fireplace.

It might seem cliché and Rockwellian, but it's what she'd always wanted. Not the enormous Greek revival mansion she'd grown up in that had felt more like a museum than a home. But that's what she and Colleen had been given and told just how grateful they should be to have the privilege.

She would have traded that "privilege" for a happy childhood any day of the week.

It said a lot to her that Sean had chosen this place to call his home. Although he hadn't come out and said it, she'd learned from the ladies at the food co-op that Sean and his friends were loaded. Really, *really* loaded. They truly were the Bachelors of Fortune.

That he'd hit the mother lode of gold strikes that day and could afford a megamansion full of the finest things but still chose to make his home in this turn-of-the-century farmhouse with its faded paint and creaky back porch stood testament to where his priorities were. And a guy who chose to live modestly wouldn't be greedy enough to resort to criminal activity, would he?

No, he wouldn't.

Her father *had* to be wrong about Sean. To be completely honest, it was beginning to feel a bit like she had been sent on a wild goose chase. Because the more she learned about Sean, the more she was convinced her father had lost his mind. During the hour she'd spent at the co-op, she'd learned that on no less than three separate occasions, Sean had dug women's cars out of the snow.

Every bit of information she uncovered pointed her further and further in the direction of Sean being nothing more than a good person. But for whatever unknown reason, Callum Charlemagne refused to believe in the possibility that there was nothing underhanded going on. It was like no other reality would make him happy.

Shannon pushed at a clump of hair that had fallen into her eye and sighed. She was just beginning to climb the stairs to look for an office or a master bedroom when she heard the sound of gravel crunching out on the drive and saw headlights pierce the dark outside. Spinning, she darted to a window and looked out in time to see Sean pulling to a stop. How her heart could soar and plummet at the same time was a complete mystery, but it did just that at the sight of him climbing from the cab of his pickup looking all rugged and sexy.

Which was all well and good until she remembered where she was. Then her anxiety shot through the roof and she looked around in a frenzy, her brain shutting down completely. She was still standing at the base of the stairs when the front door opened and Sean walked through.

His froze midstride, his face registering surprise. "What are you doing here?"

Standing around like a jackass. "I, umm, well, I needed to do laundry!" she exclaimed, feeling a fleeting sense of triumph that she'd thought of something. She tried a smile but felt it falter. "Your, uh, back door was unlocked so I let myself in. I hope that's okay."

Sean closed the door and slowly moved toward her, saying, "And what were you planning to wear while you washed your only clothes?"

Good question. "Well, I hadn't thought that far ahead, honestly." Because she hadn't considered that he would arrive home at the exact moment that she'd tried to go snooping.

He kept walking and didn't stop until he was standing within arm's reach. Expecting him to be irritated at the invasion or something, she was taken aback when his incredible green eyes went soft and warm and lazy. "I've been thinking about you," he said quietly.

The way he said it, so soft and lyrically, had her knees going weak and heat pooling in her belly. "That's nice," she whispered. "About what?"

He lowered his head until his lips were a breath away from hers and said what she'd been hoping he would because she'd been obsessing about it too. "Our kiss, lass. I've been thinking about the way you melted against me."

Mesmerized by the black stubble covering his jaw and the heat flaring to life in his gorgeous eyes, Shannon took a small step in retreat and denied weakly, "I didn't melt."

Stopping when her heels bumped the bottom stair, Shannon began to wobble and was about to fall when his hand shot out and wrapped around her waist, pulling her securely to him. "There, this is better." He murmured against her ear, his firm lips brushing her, teasing—and Shannon was in real danger of losing her composure.

How was a woman supposed to think when she was pressed against a rock-hard body like his?

Trying one last time to protest and failing miserably, Shannon simply gave up and threw caution out the window. Then she did exactly what she'd been wanting to do since the second he'd walked through the front door: she kissed him.

Refusing to think of the consequences, Shannon flung her arms around his strong, broad shoulders and covered his mouth with hers, moaning helplessly. As soon as her lips touched his, he groaned and pulled her tighter. She could feel his erection straining against her belly, hard and thick.

He tore his lips from her and rasped, "Jesus, Shannon, the things you do to me."

Riding on desire and feeling bold, she ran a hand down the flat plane of his belly to the top of his jeans and smiled when she dipped a finger inside the waistband and he hissed between his teeth. His eyes went dark emerald green and unfocused. "What do I do to you, Sean?"

He ducked his head and began kissing her neck slowly, gently. "You make me dream."

Then she melted.

Moisture pooled between her legs and she went hot and achy. No one had ever said anything like that to her before and it proved to be a potent aphrodisiac. Fisting her hands in his thick, soft hair, she found his mouth again and kissed him hard.

His tongue brushed against hers impatiently and he growled low in his throat. Then his hands were moving over her restlessly and he was tugging at the hem of her shirt, yanking until he was able to slip his palms up her ribcage and cup her breasts.

It felt incredible.

Losing all rational thought about what she was doing, Shannon moaned and arched into him. His large, hard hands were erotic torture against her sensitive skin. "Sean," she breathed.

He rolled her nipples between his fingers slowly, making her burn. "What is it, *a mhuirnin*?" he asked, his voice gone husky with need.

She wasn't exactly sure what she needed; she only knew that his touch held the answer. "I want your hands all over me."

And she got it. Sean went wild on her, stroking his hands over her now boldly, hungrily. He nipped her neck with his teeth and guided her through the room backward toward the couch as he worked his way lower. The backs of her thighs hit the cushioned arm just as his lips found her breasts and closed over one hard, sensitive peak. The friction from her cotton bra as he tongued and sucked gently had her dropping back her head and moaning.

Knowing she was losing the battle and struggling hard at that moment to care, Shannon arched into his hot mouth. "Sean." That was all she could say—just his name. All thought had drained from her brain and all that was left was the ability to feel.

"Oh, Shannon," he breathed against her, quietly, almost reverently like a scripture.

She froze. Nobody had ever said her name like that, not with so much *feeling*. It brought the reality of what they were doing crashing down on her and she shoved him away, suddenly overwhelmed. "I can't," she said, knowing that she was being a tease.

But because of her anxiety disorder, sex wasn't something she took lightly. It took a lot of trust for her to be able to relax enough to be intimate with someone—and her constant worrying made fully trusting incredibly hard. So yes, she knew she was being a horrible cocktease when she pushed away from Sean and pulled her shirt back down, her body deeply aroused and her nipples still tingling from his touch.

She knew it, and hated herself for it.

But she ran anyway.

120 JENNIFER SEASONS

Chapter Eleven

THE NEXT AFTERNOON Shannon slid quickly into an old booth at the Hole in The Wall donut bakery and hissed between her teeth, "What are you doing here?" Glancing around to make sure that nobody she recognized was in the vicinity, she brushed her hair back over her shoulder and eyed her sister suspiciously. Colleen was the last person she'd been expecting to show up.

Around a mouthful of donut, her sister replied breezily, "Checking out the local scene."

Shannon scrunched her nose in confusion. What in the hell did that mean? "Your local scene is Saratoga, not Fortune. Why did you text me? Why are you back here?"

Colleen tipped her head toward the back counter to where a college-age guy was working. Her pale blond hair shimmered gold under the bright lights. "Like I said, I've been checking out the local scene, and it's not too shabby.

Though certainly not as delectable at that Irish dream-sicle Dad sicced you on."

Craning her neck, Shannon took in the customers and the employee behind the counter, frowning when no one caught her eye. Surely her sister couldn't be referring to the college kid or the guy in a trucker's hat and coveralls sitting by the front window. On the list of fashion transgressions, his outfit had to be worse than plaid flannel. At least, one would think. Unless her sister had decided that she was now into the Ol' MacDonald type.

She turned back to Colleen. "I don't see anyone."

Her sister had crammed the rest of the donut into her mouth and was too busy chewing to respond immediately, so she held up a finger to wait. Shannon stamped down the impatience that rose up before it could grow into something a lot uglier. Something a lot like another panic attack. Having her sister show up unexpectedly had to mean something bad.

Colleen took a swig of straight black coffee, presumably to wash down the wad of donut she'd had shoved in her cheeks like a chipmunk, and burped quietly. Never let it be said that her sister was a delicate little flower. Obviously all those late-night study sessions shoving Doritos into her mouth while she memorized human anatomy had had a permanent effect on her manners. God, Mom and Dad would be proud.

"Since when did you start eating like a redneck lumberjack?"

Her sister gulped more coffee and laughed. "That sounds like a rock-band name." Then her expression changed and went tense. "But seriously, Shan, I came back because there's something I have to show yo—"

She was cut off as someone interrupted.

"You know there really is a band called Redneck Rockstars, right?" The voice came from a teenager behind Shannon who looked like a member of One Direction with his side-swept hair and skinny jeans. He was standing near another similarly dressed teen as they dumped their trays into the garbage, sending the ear buds around his neck swinging. "They're local too. Like, there're so many huge bands that have come out of Denver and the great state of Colorado in the past few years, you know? The Fray is one. And the Lumineers. I'm sure you've heard of them, right?"

Obviously music was this kid's passion. "I like them," Shannon offered. Then she felt bad about her clipped response and added, "They're about on par with Mumford and Sons, if you ask me."

The kid looked at her like she'd grown two heads and begun spouting Greek. "Um, *so* not the same."

Colleen rolled her eyes and said, "Totally different," before shooting her a wink. "As different as the Beatles from the Rolling Stones, right?"

"From who?" the kid asked, looking confused.

Shannon groaned quietly and slunk down into the booth a ways. "Oh my God, how old are we?" Since when had being twenty-nine put her into the lame-out-of-touch-old-people category?

Colleen was putting on a great act of acting casual, but Shannon could tell she was faking. Her whole body was tense. But she also must have realized the kid wasn't leaving any time soon, because Colleen just flashed the kid a big smile and said, "Tell me about these Redneck Rockstars. They sound *fascinating*."

More like the name of a really bad reality TV show, but that was just Shannon's take on things. And apparently her take was old and outdated. "Yes, fascinating," she parroted absently, though she really just wanted the kid to go away so she could figure out why the heck her sister had flown back into town. Not knowing was beginning to stir her anxiety, making her body tense and her heart rate start to speed. The part of her brain that went irrational and more than a little crazy was starting to worry that she was in big trouble over something. But that couldn't be, could it? Her father certainly hadn't said anything.

But then why else was Colleen back in Fortune?

The kid slid into the booth next to Shannon, completely ignoring her, and said to Colleen excitedly, his voice cracking in his enthusiasm, "They're from Fortune, and they're *so* good. Rumor is that they formed back in high school but one of them dropped out and stayed behind when they signed with their record label. Which makes completely no sense, right? Because, like, they're so frigging huge. Who would turn down that level of opportunity?"

The other teen piped in, a brunette girl with a super-cute pixie haircut. "I heard it was the drummer."

The Harry Styles wannabe nodded eagerly. "Right? I know, I heard that too. Like, who would do that? Who would say no to fame and fortune?"

"I totally don't know," said the brunette, her gaze locked on him. The way they were looking at each other had Shannon smiling. Ah, young insta-love. The boy left their booth suddenly without so much as a backward glance, Shannon and her sister already forgotten.

"I don't get it either," the boy continued, "but I heard the guy who stayed behind was Jake Stone, the owner of Two Moons Brewery down the street."

The girl's mouth dropped open. "Nu-uh. Shut up."

That got Shannon's attention. Sean's buddy used to be in a rock band? How funny.

Utterly absorbed in each other and their mutual passion for music, the two teens left the bakery, chattering, which left Shannon and Colleen alone again, finally.

She cut to the chase. "What are you really doing here, Colleen? No crap this time."

Colleen must have sensed Shannon was beginning to feel strung out because she sighed and said quietly, "Something's going down at home, and I needed to talk to you." Her gaze faltered and she looked away, looking a little pissy. "Okay, so maybe I missed you some too."

For Colleen that was on par with a Shakespearian sonnet, as far as confessions of the heart went. "I've missed you too, Leenie."

"For real though, I found something I'm concerned about when I pretended to clean Dad's office a few days ago. He's been locked up in there pretty much since you left. And when I have seen him, he's been abnormally preoccupied and moody, even for him. So I decided to do some snooping to find out why." She reached into the purse sitting next to her on the booth and pulled out a small black book and placed it on the table. "Take a look at this. Oh, and if things weren't already bad enough, Mom's been a mess, popping every one of her prescription pills. I even overheard her talking to her friend in San Diego about making a special trip down to Tijuana for more meds because she was so stressed out."

And that right there was why Shannon didn't medicate her anxiety. Having a walking pharmacy for a mother had soured her on the idea. It broke her heart to see how badly her mom abused her prescription drugs, and she wasn't going to run any risk that she could end up like that too. So as much as it sucked her butt big time, she dealt with her anxiety as it came.

"What do you think could be going on?" she asked as she picked up the notebook and started to flip it open to the first page.

Colleen adjusted in her seat, crossing her cargo-pant-clad legs and tugging down her snug yellow T-shirt. "You tell me. What does that look like to you?" She inclined her head toward the book, one eyebrow raised in question. Her expression was troubled.

Shannon scanned the front page, noting the four columns written in her father's handwriting. Frowning, and with a bad feeling beginning to creep up her spine, she flipped the page and read some more. Her stomach dropped.

Each page listed the same four columns: *Date, Amount Borrowed, Amount Paid,* and *Amount Still Owed.* And each page, four rows of numbers and in the right-hand margin a single word: *O'Banion.*

"Shit." She couldn't believe what she was seeing.

Colleen nodded. "That's pretty much what I said."

"These are really big numbers," Shannon said, feeling a little lightheaded all of a sudden. Wow, had it gotten hot in there? She shifted uncomfortably and tried to swallow around the lump in her throat that had magically appeared out of nowhere. It was becoming hard to breathe. *Deep, slow breaths,* she reminded herself and forced her hands to unclench.

Her sister pressed her lips together in a grim line. "Yeah, they're big numbers, all right."

As if the pages had suddenly caught fire, Shannon tossed the notebook back down on the table, unable to stand holding it any longer. "Is this what I think it is?" she asked, knowing in her gut full well that it was, but still really wanting to reject the truth.

Colleen leaned forward and nodded, her hazel eyes wide and dark with emotion. "That's Dad's secret ledger, Shan. I found it on his bookshelf shoved between Hemingway and Stegner." She took a deep breath and blurted, "I think that's his personal tab. Shannon, I think he's a gambling addict."

Shannon closed her eyes and let her head fall back against the padded booth. "Great." The truth of her sister's words rang loud and clear.

"It would make a lot of sense," Colleen insisted.

Shannon opened her eyes. "Yes, it would make sense. It would explain a lot of things. I think you're right. He's got a gambling addiction." The ledger was proof beyond a doubt. "What's O'Banion?"

"I'm not sure," her sister replied, looking conflicted. "We can't confront him, can we? I mean, what good would it do? It won't change anything. But honestly, Shannon, I wonder if this might be how we've lost all our money. You said it yourself, those numbers are huge."

Because that lump was still firmly lodged in her throat, Shannon just nodded. What she didn't get was why her father had sent her to Sean if he was in debt from gambling. What did Sean have to do with anything? She didn't know, but she sure didn't like this new turn of events. Not one little bit.

Swallowing hard, she finally managed to say, "I need time to think this through."

Her sister nodded. "That's why I needed to show you. You're more perceptive than me." Then she added, "But I'm damn good at research. And I can smell something funny about this whole Muldoon thing. I don't like that Dad has you tangled up in it—especially if it's somehow connected to this," she finished, tapping the black ledger with a finger.

Loving that protective side of Colleen and feeling thankful for the connection, Shannon grabbed her sister's hand and squeezed it tight. "I love you, Leenie."

"I love you too," Colleen said, returning the affection. She took a deep breath, adding, "And that's why I'm not going back home yet. I told Mom and Dad that I started my internship in Boston early, so they're not expecting me back for a few weeks. I'm going to stick around here and do my own snooping."

Wanting to protest but really liking the idea of having her sister close by, Shannon gave her hand one last squeeze and let it go. "That's not necessary," she said half-heartedly.

Colleen gave her a level look. "It is. My instincts are up, Shannon, and I'm not okay leaving you out here all alone until I know exactly what the hell is going on. But don't worry, I'll do my thing and keep my distance so I don't stir up any suspicion. If I find anything out, I'll let you know."

Not a hundred percent sure if that was the best plan or not, but really, really glad for the support, Shannon smiled gratefully. "Sounds good. It's comforting knowing you'll be close by."

With eyes dark and intense with emotion, Colleen said, "I love you more than anyone in this messed-up family. I'm not going to let anything happen to you." Then she pasted on a bright smile and gestured around the donut shop. "Besides, I get a nice little vacation out of it here in the great West. I'm not complaining."

Shannon could tell she was trying to lighten the mood and was thankful. She could use a few minutes of levity.

The doorbell over the donut shop door jangled as a customer entered. Or she thought it was a customer. The guy was big and bad and looked hella sexy. Actually, more precisely, he looked like a rock star. She couldn't stop her mouth from dropping open, her problems momentarily overshadowed by the jarring sight of him. The guy had tattoos all over his arms, pierced ears, and leather bracelets on his wrists. And he wore a snug black T-shirt over his tough, muscled body with frayed jeans. As he passed them, heading straight to the back of the bakery, he removed some badass-looking sunglasses and Shannon caught a glimpse of gorgeous baby blues.

Colleen sputtered, "Holy shit, did you see that guy?"

How could she not? "Maybe he's one of those band members back for a visit?" Shannon was only half-joking. He certainly looked the part.

Craning her neck, Colleen almost fell out of the booth and scrambled back into her seat. "But why would he go in the back like he works here?"

Although a big part of her wanted to forget reality and sink into a gossip-fest with her sister about the guy, it was getting late, there was a ton to do, and Shannon was really feeling the pressure. "I have no idea. You could follow him and find out."

Because her sister made a move like she was going to do exactly that, scooting toward the edge of the booth, Shannon rushed to say, "But don't! You can't go back there."

Colleen leveled her with a stare. "I'm a grown woman, honey. I can do what I want."

True. But it might result in her getting kicked out of a donut shop. "Please don't. Look, how about this. When everything is back to normal, we'll come back to Colorado for a vacation. Not here, obviously. But, we'll go somewhere full of rugged mountain men—just for you."

"Sounds like a plan," Colleen agreed, resettling in her seat. "I'm liking what I see of these Colorado guys. We could come back and do a tasting tour." The way she said it left no room for doubt about what she meant.

Too bad there was only one man Shannon was currently interested in tasting, and he was off limits. There wasn't going to be a repeat of last night. There couldn't be.

Just then, the very man she was thinking about strolled by the front window of the bakery, looking sinful and so very Irish with his wool cap. Her heart leapt into her throat at the very sight of him and her stomach got all jittery. And when he smiled at an older couple he passed, tipping his cap, she felt the heat of it clear down to her toes. Wow, that man was potent.

Too bad he wasn't hers and never would be.

THAT SAME AFTERNOON back at Pine Creek, Sean had just spotted Shannon near the pastures watching the foals with a foot propped on the bottom fence rail. The expression on her face was soft and content, and it made his chest squeeze. Watching her as he made his way between the barns toward the big meadow, Sean took in the way her hair glimmered copper in the sunlight, and her body leaned forward over the fence to give some grass to a curious foal. Seeing her there with his horses made something shift inside him and go warm and gooey. Shite.

"I was beginning to think you were avoiding me," he said when he reached her side. Last night's kiss came rushing back to him, searing his brain with the hot memory.

Shannon looked over at him and her smile fell. "I'm sorry, Sean."

"It was just a mad case of blue balls ye left me with, not to worry." Though he was joking, it'd been the truth. And taking care of it had barely satiated his need. Shannon was one seriously desirable woman.

Her face went red as a cherry tomato. "Oh, my gosh, I'm so sorry."

Seeing that she looked upset and was beginning to get all fidgety, Sean leaned his elbows on the top fence rail and braced a foot too. "No big thing." Although it was—it was a very big thing—but he wanted her to relax and feel safe, so he kept it casual. Why he cared so much, he didn't understand. He only knew that he felt a rising need to protect her.

Whatever the reason, he was beginning to suspect that it wasn't going to go away anytime soon. And that was a real problem, because after what had happened at Belmont, he was more convinced than ever that it was best to leave her alone. Despite their kiss last night. Call it a moment of weakness, but he hadn't been able to resist. Coming home and seeing her standing there like she'd been waiting for him had stirred his desire uncontrollably.

But he had to control it—for her sake. "So, about last night," he began as one of Zeke's new offspring, a bay filly with a giant blaze on her face and a stocking that reached her fetlock, went ripping past, bucking and frolicking. Sean couldn't help smiling when Shannon grinned at the filly. It lit up her whole face. Then she glanced at him out of the corner of her eye, and he damn near missed his landing when he switched feet.

"It won't happen again. It's too complicated." The words were soft and, if he wasn't mistaken, intermixed with the slightest hint of disappointment.

That made two of them.

But it was the way it had to be. "Agreed." It was the right thing to do. Still, he wasn't going to pretend it didn't suck big bollocks.

Shannon cleared her throat, and he got distracted admiring the way her auburn hair contrasted against the paleness of her skin. Christ, she was pretty.

"Now that we've settled that, tell me about you, Sean. What was it like growing up in Dublin?" She brushed back a strand of loose hair and smiled. "Besides the whole boxing thing."

Sean thought about it for a minute, trying to figure out how best to phrase things. He'd not had the best, most stable upbringing. "Well, let's see," he started. "I was raised by me mum who was an actress and worked mostly at the Gate Theatre. We lived in a tiny little flat that was situated above a pub in the Temple Bar district. She always wanted to move us to New York and act on Broadway, but died of breast cancer before I turned eighteen."

Her brown eyes brimmed with sympathy. "I'm so sorry. That's tough. What about your dad?"

That had him scoffing. "What da?"

"You didn't have a father growing up?" Sean appreciated the lack of judgment in her voice. He'd dealt with enough pity to last a lifetime on that score.

Sean shook his head and watched another foal nudge its mother with its nose to nurse while she grazed peacefully on the tall green grass. "I didn't, no." A laugh caught in his chest and he let it loose. "Funny story, actually. I didn't know who the man even was until he died a few years back. Somebody tried contacting me mum to tell her, but with her being dead already, the information eventually found its way to me. It was the first time I learned his name."

Her expression was horrified. "That's not funny, that's awful."

Tomato, tomahto. He shrugged, his tone light. "It took a while, but I'm over it now. I've learned that it never does any good to stay angry. And that's not the funny part. When I heard about him, I left here and went to Philadelphia, to his home. And when I was there, I met a man who turned out to be my half-brother."

"You're kidding me!" Her mouth dropped open in the cutest way. Made him want to kiss it shut.

"Totally serious. You might have heard of him actually. His name is Peter Kowalskin."

This time, her foot slipped off the bottom fence rung and she gaped at him. "You mean the famous baseball player? The one that played for the Denver Rush before retiring?"

Sean gave her a wink. The look of shock on her face was adorable. "That's the one. His mum was Irish too, apparently. As Peter told it to me over a pint of Gat, she left our da when Peter was just a babe and moved back to Ireland. Our da came looking for her and that's when he met me mum instead. They had a poke together before he went back to Philadelphia. The guy never knew about me."

Shannon placed a hand on his chest and the heat of it melted into him. "That's about the saddest thing I've ever heard." Her eyes were big and wet with unshed tears.

"Don't go soft on me, Shannon," he replied with warning. He wouldn't be able to handle it if she did. Seeing her cry would undo him. "I've not had the best upbringing, but I survived and have a good life now. In the end, that's all that matters."

She dropped her hand, much to his disappointment, and resumed her spot on the fence watching the frolicking foals. "I hear you. It's not where you come from, but where you go and what you build that matters." She looked over her shoulder at the barns and then back to him. "You've built something to be proud of, Sean."

He really had. He had built this really great life—and now there was this amazing woman before him. If he were a normal man, this would be a no-brainer. But that was the bitch of it. Normal men weren't living on borrowed time like he was. Bracing his foot on the bottom rung again, he couldn't help but wonder how long it was all going to last.

Suddenly she leaned into him and gave him a good nudge with her shoulder. When he looked down, she was staring straight ahead. "I have to confess something," she said.

"What's that?" Christ, even the way she scrunched her freckled nose was cute too.

She sighed, long and slow—like what she was about to say pained her. "I shouldn't, but I really like you, Sean."

It hit him. Right between the rib cage. It felt like being sucker punched in the kidney—only a hell of a lot more winding.

Taking a steadying breath of his own, Sean nudged her back and replied, "I really like you too, Shannon."

If only.

"Come to the pub with me tonight," he said, the invitation popping out before he could stop and think. Holding his breath, he waited anxiously for her response. Because now that he *had* said it, he wanted her to say yes.

Like she knew the wait was killing him inside, she took her sweet time answering. "As friends?"

"Of course," he replied automatically.

Finally, she glanced at him out of the corner of her eyes and smiled gently. "Sure. That sounds nice."

The air rushed from his lungs and he inhaled deep. In his world, *nice* didn't even come close to describing it.

It sounded like heaven.

Chapter Twelve

SHANNON WASN'T CALLING it a date—because it wasn't a date. Sean might have asked her out for a pint at Two Moons, and she may have said yes—but it still wasn't a date. There was a whole connotation there that she wasn't comfortable with.

But she couldn't deny that it felt kind of good to walk into the brewpub with Sean and have the ladies eye her with envy. Only she was keeping that little secret. What she felt and how she chose to act were very different things. She could think whatever she wanted to about Sean, but she was staying completely hands-off and not *doing* anything.

Or *anyone*.

Sean led her to a booth against the far wall with windows that overlooked the huge brick patio. Double glass doors opened onto it, and Shannon could hear the sound of water rushing from the waterfall feature that sat smack in the center of the outdoor entertaining space, surrounded by tall grasses and echinacea. The sun had just set and the tables out there were packed with pubgoers soaking up the gorgeous summer evening and surrounded by lit Tiki torches.

A few dozen more people were milling around inside the open-raftered pub, chatting casually and listening to the jukebox shift through tunes. Tonight, for whatever reason, nineties grunge was the thing. It was too bad Colleen wasn't there; she'd have been going crazy with all these guys digging on Nirvana and Pearl Jam. Though many of them weren't actually doing so, she could tell that in their hearts they were all lighting cigarettes, growing their hair long—and her sister's personal favorite—wearing flannel. Long live Kurt Cobain, man.

"Here, why don't you take this side?" Sean said to her. "I'll grab us a few pints and be right back."

Shannon smiled and sat down. She'd worn her hair loose tonight and tossed it over her shoulder. "Sure thing." It would give her a few minutes to have a better look around anyway. Still, she shamelessly scoped out his backside as he made his way through the crowd toward the bar where Jake was busy bartending and getting hit on by the ladies. It was easy to see why, now that she had a clear look at him. The guy was gorgeous, in that gruff, masculine kind of way. And when he chose to bring out his smile, it was almost brutalizing in its raw sex appeal.

This guy used to be in a rock band? Yeah, she could see it. He had that quality about him. Huh. Maybe she should go ask him about that Hole in The Wall guy after all. See if he knew anything. Because *that* man had to be an anomaly.

Or maybe, more importantly, she should find out what he was willing to share about Sean. See if she could turn up anything. Although at this point, she was pretty certain that there was nothing to find. And deep down, she was glad. She wanted to believe in his innocence.

Then a thought occurred to her that she didn't like. Was she not finding anything because she'd already made up her mind that Sean was innocent? Was she not even really trying?

Before she could ride that train farther down its track, Sean arrived back at their table with a pitcher of beer and two glasses. "I forgot what night it is. You're in for a treat, Shannon. Jake's about to gear up the karaoke machine." The grin he gave her was completely unguarded and full of good humor—and hot enough to make a girl weak in the knees. Wow.

Tongue stuck to the roof of her mouth like an infatuated idiot, Shannon finally pried it back down and managed, "I'm a terrible singer."

Sliding into the seat across from her, Sean laughed good-naturedly. "Oh, not for you, lass. We good people of Fortune adore our Saturday night karaoke. It's everyone's chance to be an American Idol. And, well, we drunkards in our seats make a very supportive and enthusiastic audience. It's quite fecking funny."

She could use some funny. Real funny. Not the type of funny like he'd talked about earlier. That had just been heartbreaking.

Shannon took a sip of her beer and said, "Then by all means, have at it, slugger."

"Not even a chance," was all he said, his green eyes dancing.

Before she could respond, she spotted someone. "Hey, Apple's here."

The woman under discussion stopped at their table. "Hi, you two." Then she looked at Shannon. "I'm here to take your advice."

Shannon felt her eyebrows rise and quickly composed them. "Wow. Well, that's great. What are you going to do?" The librarian certainly wasn't dressed for naughty in her modest vintage print dress and eyelet cardigan. And those eyeglasses. She was so retro-hip it was awesome—like those models on Etsy. Although Apple didn't strike her as the kind of woman who dressed that way to be trendy. It was just how she was. And that's what made her all the more fabulous. Authenticity.

Something Shannon herself was really struggling with at the moment. For crissakes, she couldn't even be real with her parents. How was that for maturity?

Shaking off the unsettling thought, Shannon tuned back in just as the blond replied, "First I'm going to have something to eat and a beer. I don't normally drink," she said aiming a frown over her shoulder toward Jake, "but I've been building up a tolerance lately trying to get that jerk's attention long enough for an interview."

Just then a tall, auburn-haired guy with a mischievous grin walked up behind her and said, "So you can hold down, what, an entire beer now?" Obviously they knew each other.

Sean spoke up then, chuckling. "Give the lass a break, Aidan. And meet Shannon, my new stable manager."

The good-looking guy leaned around Apple and stretched out a hand. "Nice to meet you, Shannon. I'm Aidan."

She shook his hand. "Likewise. I've heard a lot about you."

"It must all be lies then." He laughed and straightened.

Sean broke into a crooked grin. "Don't flatter yourself."

Aidan placed his hands on Apple's softly rounded shoulders and began to rub gently, his attention on Sean. Were he and Apple dating?

"How long have you two been together?" Shannon asked.

They both stopped dead, looking startled. For a suspended moment they just stared at her in blank shock. And then they started laughing.

Apple shook her head. "We're not together, honey. We're family. This big loon is my cousin."

Really? Man, there was absolutely no family resemblance. Oh wait, no, there it was. If she looked hard enough she could see it around the eyes and mouth. "I'm so sorry."

Aidan shrugged it off. "No prob."

Sean was looking between the two, his face registering surprise. "Why have I lived here the past five years now, and I never knew you were related?"

The two cousins looked at each other and then back at Sean, shrugging as if they clearly thought it was obvious. Like, *duh*. Anyone with a set of eyes in their head should be able to see the resemblance.

Aidan glanced at Sean. "Got room at the table for one more?"

The Irishman sighed and then said, "Sure, mate."

Was that hesitation? Did he just hesitate? *Ooh*, was he reluctant to share their booth? The thought that he might be gave her butterflies. She chewed her bottom lip to hide the smile currently forming at the idea that he might want to be alone with her. She'd take that.

Aidan sat down next to Sean, and Shannon found herself directly opposite two incredibly good-looking men. One dark and gorgeous and a little tough. The other rugged and outdoorsy. Jesus. Was there something in the Fortune drinking water that made everyone there look amazing? If so, she was moving there in a heartbeat. She could use some amazing. Maybe then she'd be more than mediocre at everything.

Apple spoke up, excusing herself. "I'm going to grab a seat at the bar." She placed a hand on Shannon's shoulder, looking down at her. "We'll talk later?"

Shannon nodded and smiled, suddenly feeling shy— which was weird. It was just that Apple treated her like a real friend, and they barely knew each other. Was it a small-town thing?

Shannon watched her friend go and couldn't help but notice the frown that overtook Jake's face the minute he spotted Apple. Boy, she hadn't been kidding about his perma-scowl, had she? But that didn't stop her. Nope, the voluptuous librarian plopped herself on an open bar stool and signaled for a drink.

Go get him, girl.

It was odd that she felt so invested in Apple's little struggle, but she did. She wanted her new friend to triumph. Maybe in part because she needed to know it was possible to overcome adversity—and maybe in part because the woman was simply a doll and deserved his cooperation.

"How do you like Fortune, Shannon?" Aidan asked.

Reluctantly dragging her gaze from the drama that was about to play out at the bar, Shannon gave him a friendly smile, well aware that Sean's eyes were on her. She could feel his gaze almost like a physical force. "It's absolutely beautiful," she replied, swallowing hard. She hated being under scrutiny. Though to be fair, Aidan's question wasn't scrutinizing—it was normal and friendly. It was more that she was beginning to worry that her true objectives for being in Fortune were becoming horribly transparent.

Aidan smiled back, easy and carefree. "It is that. I was born and raised here and can't imagine making my home anywhere else." Something fleeting shadowed his gaze, dimming it, but then it cleared again like it had never passed through in the first place. She wondered at it briefly.

A waitress showed up then and they ordered. By the time the food came, the first pitcher of beer had been emptied—mostly by Sean and Aidan. The two were laughing and joking and having a great time. It made Shannon wonder what it would be like to have a friend like that. Someone who wasn't also her sister and could make her crazy.

For the next hour they were entertained by karaoke singers with varying degrees of talent. Though it seemed like the more they drank, the worse they actually sang, but the louder the audience became. Same with the applause. By the time they'd finished eating, the place was jam-packed full of people clapping so hard and whistling so shrilly that it felt like being at a real live concert. Boy, Sean hadn't been kidding.

Fortune had spirit.

Not for the first time, Shannon felt a yearning deep down inside her and wondered what it would be like to belong to such a community. To have people genuinely care and want to get to know her. To be accepted and to feel a part of something she could believe in and be proud of.

God, wouldn't that be something?

For the slightest hint of a second, Shannon let herself imagine living in Fortune. Maybe she'd get a little place in town, date Sean. Oh, and maybe she'd open up her riding school. Horses were amazing, but competitive jumping stank. It had never been what she'd wanted to do with her life. But she could see it now—all of it out at Pine Creek Ranch. Just a small riding school, where she could give group and individual lessons to children of all ages and abilities.

That would be so great.

At that moment, an ear-piercing screech came from the microphone. Shannon cringed, Sean swore, and all of them turned to the small karaoke stage at the back wall. Apple was up there, looking flushed and more than a little glassy-eyed. She tapped the mic again and hiccupped before slurring, "Testing, testing. One, two, three."

Good gravy, the woman looked wasted.

But if anyone was worried about it, they sure weren't showing it. Nope. Not even close.

Aidan placed his fingers in his mouth and whistled loud enough to break Shannon's eardrums. "You do it, girl!"

Sean looked at his friend, his eyebrows high in surprise. "You think she's really going to do it?"

"Do what?" Shannon asked, totally in the dark.

"Apple has a fear of public speaking," Aidan replied with a wide grin. "But she's pissed as the wind right now and I think she might actually sing. It'll be good for her."

Right.

But somehow she doubted it.

Shannon glanced around the crowded brewpub and stopped on Jake when she saw his expression. He looked anything but happy. In fact, if he scowled any more, his face might be in danger of permanently cramping. And his frown was aimed directly at Apple.

Tapping the mic again as music began to play, Apple swiped a hand under her nose and sniffed loudly, her bun now lopsided and loose, her enormous glasses slipping down her nose. "Here's to all you people out there tonight who, like me, have been done wrong by some dirty dog."

Suddenly, sounding downright surly, Jake hollered, "Watch yourself, girl."

Apple squinted her eyes and pointed a finger at him sloppily. "No, *you* watch yourself, Jake Stone! I'm a'gonna sing." And then she flung her arms up in a flamboyant gesture, ramming the mic into the wall behind her and causing a horrible sound.

Sean scratched his chin and sounded impressed. "That lass is *totally* wrecked."

Yeah, she was. One shoulder of her cardigan had fallen off, now draped around her elbow, and apparently she'd lost her shoes because she was barefoot. "I couldn't agree more. Should we do something?"

Aidan shook his head. "Let her have this."

So she did, even though she was worried. Shannon sat back in her seat as Apple opened her mouth and started singing that old R.E.M. song "Everybody Hurts." And then she cringed. It was the worst singing she'd ever heard in her life.

Apple was up on stage with her eyes closed, one hand cradling the mic stand to her while she wailed into the microphone with all her might about taking comfort from her friends and holding on. It was so bad it was just, well, painful.

But soon, the crowd started cheering her on, calling out to her. And really, why wouldn't they? Shannon had never seen anyone commit to a song the way Apple was doing. That woman was doing it with *feeling*. Before long, lighters came out, raised in the air, turning the pub into a united front of support for the town librarian. And then they were singing along too, swaying together like branches in the breeze. It was amazing.

The woman was butchering the song and her town loved her for it.

Turning her head, Shannon caught sight of Jake and a surprised laugh escaped her. Quickly she turned back to Sean and Aidan. "Hey, you two, look." She tipped her head in the bar owner's direction.

They did and both their faces froze in shock. Because there was Jake, white bar towel flung over his shoulder, lighter fired up and waving in the air. He caught them all staring openly at him and shrugged his broad shoulders.

Clearly even he couldn't resist Apple's awesomeness.

Chapter Thirteen

THREE DAYS LATER, Sean went to a small celebration. Every year on the anniversary of the gold strike, the day that they'd all gotten so damn lucky, he and the guys got together at Jake's place to commemorate the event. They'd meet in the afternoon and sit on the back porch of his cabin that overlooked the river. Then they'd share a few of those beers that they'd got pissed on before having their dreams come true.

Pulling his Ford to a stop in the drive behind Jake's classic restored '72 GMC pickup, he noted that Aidan was already there. His Tundra was parked off to the right behind a big woodshed, a huge pile of lumber jutting off the long-bed and held down with bungee ties.

Not even bothering with the front door, Sean made his way around the side of the old-fashioned log cabin and ducked under the low-hanging branches of a monstrous pine tree. Cones crunched under his work boots as he made his way to the raised back porch. When he spotted Aidan and Jake, they were already kicked back in camp chairs and enjoying the view of the river just past the small stand of trees.

"Happy anniversary," Sean said in greeting as he climbed the stairs to join them. "You lucky feckin' bastards."

Both the guys laughed and raised the beer bottles they were already holding. "Damn straight," Jake said and tossed an unopened bottle to him. "You being the luckiest bastard of us all, what with your obscenely large gold-nugget score."

Wasn't that the bloody truth? He'd pulled the biggest chunk by far out of the river that day. Sean pulled up the third camp chair and took a seat. "I'll drink to that." But he hadn't felt right about his being the most valuable piece, so he'd convinced them to pool together and split the payout equally among them. Still, they liked to tease him about the size of his nugget once in a while. He popped the cap before raising the bottle to meet theirs and said with no little amount of irony, "To the Bachelors of Fortune."

They tapped bottles, took long drinks, and then sat in appreciative silence. Though they made light of it the vast majority of the time, that day had changed everything for them all. Coming back to the spot where fortune had tipped her hand to them so generously was moving. That day had given them all something profoundly personal— it had given them hope.

Jake was the first to break the silence. "Your stable manager is attractive." His hair was pulled back in its usual stubby ponytail under a navy blue ski cap, and he hadn't shaved in days, likely since Sean had last seen him. He'd often thought it fitting that his mate lived in a rustic cabin because he couldn't think of anyone better suited to that lifestyle than Jake.

Sean smirked. "She is that."

Aidan kicked out his long legs covered in utility cargos and crossed his heavy boots, one over the other. Then he raised his arms and laced his fingers together behind his head, grinning. "Come on, man. We know you're into her. It was obvious by the dumb look on your face when Apple sang the other night at the bar."

Jake groaned under his breath irritably. "Don't remind me."

Ignoring him, Sean leaned back more comfortably in his chair and sighed, confessing, "I'd like to, mate, but it's not going to happen. Too messy."

Aidan gave a *hmph* and grumbled. "It always is. They just won't let it be any other way." The way he said it made it sound like he had a whole lot of personal experience.

"Who got you all tangled up, mate?"

Aidan's hazel eyes went dark. "I don't want to talk about it."

Jake looked over at him, his beer bottle halfway to his lips. "Why, because the thought of her still pisses you off that much?"

"So what if it does?"

Jake held Aidan's gaze steady. "Because it was a long time ago, man—and because you gotta move on at some point."

"You don't think I haven't?" Aidan shot back. "Fuck that, dude. You know I've had plenty of girlfriends since my college days."

Jake sighed and rolled his eyes skyward like he was suffering silently and praying for patience. "That's not what I mean, and you know it. But whatever, man. If you want to keep wasting your time being heartbroken over a woman who didn't want you, then by all means. Be an ass."

Changing the topic before things got heated, Sean asked a question that had been bothering him. "Why'd you stand Apple up that day a few weeks back, Jake? You know she didn't deserve that."

With a curse, his friend rose from his chair and paced away. The back of his long sleeved T-shirt had a list of cities and dates on them. Looking closer, Sean saw that it was a list of tour dates for Jake's old band, Redneck Rockstars, and grinned. It was a damn funny name.

"I had to help my dad out, okay?" Jake finally admitted. "He'd gone on one of his benders again and fallen into the hay shoot out on Mill Road. You know, that rusty old one that some rancher abandoned on the side of the road years ago?"

Both Sean and Aidan nodded.

He continued, his mouth drawn in a tight line. "Polly Silts saw him and called me. He was passed out by the time I got to him and had a nasty gash on his head, so I brought him back here and fixed him up, because you know how he is about hospitals. I've given up trying to get him to go and just learned how to stitch him up myself." He pegged them with a stare. "Don't tell anyone. Especially not Apple. Promise me."

It was widely known that Jake's dad was the town drunk. Verle Stone had gained that title through good old-fashioned binge drinking and public intoxication—and a whole lot of trashy behavior. It was a cross that Jake had to bear.

Aidan nodded and said quietly, "We won't say anything, man. I'm sorry about your dad. Is he okay now?"

Jake gave a weary sigh and leaned against the porch railing, "He's the same as he ever was."

That pretty much summed up everything.

Knowing it, Aidan hitched his thumb over his shoulder and smirked at Jake. "I meant to say something earlier, but your place is a shit pit, man. When was the last time you cleaned it?"

Jake grinned lightning fast, unoffended. "You offering, neat freak?"

"Not in this lifetime."

"Why not, sissy? I've seen you in an apron. You're sexy."

"That was Home Ec in eighth grade, idiot."

"Still counts."

Realizing the guys could be at it for a while, Sean kicked back in his seat and nursed his bottle of ale, his mind wandering. It wasn't until Aidan kicked him in the shin that he came to. "Hey, where you been? Man, you're as bad lately as Ben Stiller in that Walter Mitty movie. I asked how Zeke was doing."

"Recovering well." The relief he still felt about that was palpable. Shannon had taken a personal interest and had been doing an amazing job caring for him, for which he was eternally grateful. She definitely had a way. "He won't be able to run again, but he can still sire with the use of in vitro—which we've been using more of lately anyway. The tendon that was severed won't allow for him to ever stretch out enough to mount a mare again." Whoever had harmed the stallion must not have realized that by making him lame permanently and forcing in vitro, his breeding fee had just skyrocketed. Zeke's injury had ironically made him more valuable than the multimillion-dollar Triple Crown winner already was.

It would objectively be a good thing, if it weren't so worrisome. Now that his fee was going to surge, whoever had attacked him wasn't going to be happy. Sean was beginning to worry for his horse's safety, even at home. Was the arsehole willing to go so far on Sean's home turf? He hoped to hell not, but he wasn't willing to bet on it.

Then again, there was no proof that Zeke's injury was intentional. And his own attack? Well, for all he actually bloody well knew, a clumsy stable hand who'd panicked and run off could have accidentally clanged him in the head with a shovel. Maybe he was just imagining the whole fecking thing.

The Irish mob hadn't tracked him down.

Zeke wasn't being targeted.

Nobody had knocked him senseless on purpose.

There wasn't a cock-shouldered Irish thug running about trying to put a hit on him.

And most importantly: He wasn't falling hard for a woman he couldn't even confess his real last name to out of fear for her safety.

Nope. Not at all. Not even bloody fecking close.

Bollocks.

Chapter Fourteen

SHANNON LEFT HER apartment and went downstairs to the main floor of the barn, her father's voice still ringing in her ears. The phone call they'd just shared had really been a one-sided verbal lashing. Callum Charlemagne was gravely disappointed in his daughter.

What else was new?

Struggling against the tension gripping her body like a boa constrictor, Shannon made her way to the storage room with the huge metal cabinet she wanted to search at the base of the stairs. If she didn't find something *today*, her father was pulling the rug out from under Colleen. It was all on Shannon's shoulders to make sure that didn't happen.

Talk about feeling the pressure.

It boggled her mind that he would even consider doing such a thing to his own child, but she supposed she could look at it as a testament to the gravity of the situation.

Taking a deep, calming breath, Shannon reminded herself that his world was on the brink of collapse. It wasn't overly surprising that her father was stressed and lashing out.

"Doesn't mean I deserve it, though," she said to no one in particular. But it helped sometimes to talk out loud and give a direction to her frantically racing thoughts. Being forced to concentrate on forming words was sometimes enough to break the cycle.

If nothing else, it gave her company.

Just then, the barn door creaked open and Tim Hopkins, the yearling trainer, entered. He smiled a friendly greeting when he spotted Shannon. "Good morning," he said. "I'm just swinging by to grab some topical antibiotic for Grey's hip. He and another yearling got into it out in the paddock and a small chunk got taken out of him."

Ouch. That didn't sound pleasant. But since she was going into the room anyway to try and pick the cabinet lock with a hairpin, Shannon smiled back and offered, "Why don't I grab it for you? I was just headed in there anyway."

The older man nodded, looking thankful. "That'd be great, actually. I'm dying for the bathroom."

The rational part of her brain saw the opportunity and took it. Before he could change his mind and decided he could hold it longer, Shannon held out her hand. "Can I borrow your key, please?"

Tim looked at her with mild surprise. "Sean hasn't made you one yet?" She shook her head. "Huh. That's odd."

Smiling weakly, Shannon snatched the keys out of his hand and tried for breezy. "Do your thing. I've got this." Now she really wanted to know why she hadn't gotten a key. Was there something in the cabinet she wasn't supposed to know about?

"Don't be silly," she mumbled under her breath as she worked the lock. He was simply busy, that's all. But the vague nagging worry wouldn't completely go away, no matter how many deep, steadying breaths she took.

"I'll be right back!" Tim hollered from the barn entrance.

She glanced out the window at the bright blue patch of sky. "Sounds good!" she yelled back, the lock finally giving.

Relieved, but still way jittery, Shannon swung the cabinet doors wide open with a creak and spent a few minutes looking inside. Medical supplies were stacked and lined in neat rows, grouped together according to use. Bandages were together in a basket, unopened vaccines that didn't need to be refrigerated were clumped together, and various bottles of pills and ointments were arranged neatly on another shelf. Spotting the topical ointment that Tim would need, Shannon's hand stopped midreach when she noticed something peculiar. Up on the top shelf were a bunch of bottles that had a very fine layer of dust on them. Shannon leaned closer and rose on her tippy-toes for a better peek. And noticed a slight circular ring on the shelf where a bottle had once been—a bottle of something had been sitting there just recently.

Then something else caught her eye.

"Hey, Tim, are you there?" she said loudly with her head shoved deep in the cabinet. She thought she'd heard footsteps signaling his return, but it was hard to tell with the metal muffling all noise. "There's a disposable syringe wrapper sitting here on the shelf opened and empty. Did somebody get a shot recently?" Unease crept up her spine and she went tense again. Why, she wasn't sure. A wrapper alone wasn't cause for alarm. But there was that dust ring too.

Tim stepped into the doorway, his white bushy eyebrows pulled down in confusion. "Not that I know of, no."

Shannon held up the wrapper, her pulse skittering. Something wasn't setting right with her about this, but it was probably just because she'd spent an hour getting her ass chewed by her father for being too naïve. He'd accused her of not being able to recognize suspicious activity if she tripped over it, even though she'd spent the past weeks doing nothing else but searching for that very thing. The only place she hadn't managed to get to again was Sean's house. But she was avoiding that place.

Because it was far too tempting, that house. It made her want to do very fun but very wrong things with the man who owned it. And since she didn't trust that she'd be able keep her hands off him if they were alone again, she'd stayed away, no matter how much her father threatened.

Well, she hadn't tripped over it, so to speak, but these missing things qualified as suspicious. And she'd noticed. *Take that, Dad.*

Mad now at his mistreatment of her and with her ego still stinging, Shannon grabbed the tube of ointment and squeezed briefly. Then she remembered that she was supposed to be getting something too and snagged a jar of Bag Balm off the shelf.

"Is everything okay?" Tim said suddenly from behind her, clearly noticing her preoccupation.

Even though her stomach squeezed painfully with unease, she quickly slammed the cabinet shut, trying not to let her imagination grab hold and make her think all kinds of crazy, silly things. So a bottle and a syringe were missing? Big deal. It didn't have to mean anything.

Walking quickly to the trainer, Shannon handed him the tube and his keys. "There you are," she said with fake cheer, because her insides were spinning, making her slightly nauseated. "I'll walk you out." Some fresh air right then sounded heavenly.

Tim tipped his head down the main aisle to the big double doors that were swung wide open to capture the morning breeze. "I was going to go out that way. It's closer to the paddock."

Though her heart was beating heavily and it was hard to swallow, she forced her shoulders to relax and tried hard to bring her thoughts into focus. "Sounds great," she said, putting the jar down quickly on a hay bale when his head was turned. And then started walking, Tim falling into step beside her.

"So how are you liking Pine Creek?" he asked.

Glancing at the empty stalls they passed, Shannon replied after a steadying breath. "It's wonderful." There was no harm in being truthful about that. Pine Creek was quickly grabbing hold of her heart and claiming a spot, just like its owner.

Tim puffed his chest out, clearly proud. "Couldn't agree more. I came to work for Sean right after he bought this place, and I'm amazed at what he's created in such a short time. His breeding program is top notch, and these horses are some of the fastest I've seen." He smiled like a proud father before continuing. "I've wondered about Zeke's bloodlines because I've never seen a stronger, swifter runner, but all that Sean's told me is that he's from Irish Thoroughbred stock."

Shannon's eyebrows rose in surprise. "You haven't seen his pedigree?"

Tim shook his head. "Everything's been word of mouth. I'm told they go clear back to Shergar."

Her mouth dropped open in disbelief and she stopped dead in her tracks. "Are you kidding me?" That horse was a famous Irish Derby winner.

"Not even slightly," Tim said, chuckling heartily. He was clearly amused by her shocked response.

"But wasn't he kidnapped or something after a record-breaking race back in the early eighties? she asked, suddenly puzzled by the story she thought she remembered from her childhood. If it was correct, he'd been taken for ransom but was never actually seen again.

Tim looked impressed with her knowledge of horseracing lore, but that incident was legendary in the racing world, even though it had happened clear across the Atlantic. "Yeah, that's right. He was stolen at gunpoint by masked men."

It was one of those stories that was almost too incredible to believe.

Shannon laughed a little, amazed. "I can't believe it. Zeke is one of his grandbabies?" No wonder Sean loved that horse so much. Shergar's coveted bloodline had supposedly died out after he'd been stolen. If it was true, that stallion was beyond priceless.

Tim nodded. "That's what I've heard. Impressive, isn't it?"

Shannon wondered if her dad knew this information about Zeke. And then she decided probably not; otherwise, he wouldn't be so convinced Sean was doping his horses. If that stallion's bloodlines were present, then there was no foul play—it was simply in Zeke's genes to fly. And luckily for Sean, Shergar'd passed that winning trait on to his offspring.

Shannon quickly compiled a new version of events in her mind, one she liked much more, and suddenly felt better about things. There was no wrongdoing. Just a legendary bloodline, thought lost, but was actually still in existence and stronger now than the industry had seen in over thirty years.

No wonder her father was suspicious. Suspicious—but completely and totally wrong. *Thank goodness.*

She refused to consider why she felt such a fervent need to believe her new truth. She just did.

Relief flooded her, but the reprieve was short-lived. As they reached the last stall, Shannon glanced in briefly and kept walking. Until what she'd just seen registered. Then she spun back around and dashed to the gate. A sob broke out when she saw what was inside.

Tim rushed to her side. "What is it?"

Shannon stared blankly, on the verge of tears. They welled up inside her. "Look." It was all she could manage to say. How could this be?

Tim came up next to her and looked inside, swearing instantly. Violently. "Stay back," he ordered and opened the stall gate.

She couldn't have moved even if she wanted to. Her eyes were locked on the horror before her. "Is she breathing?" she whispered.

Tim took the few steps necessary and crouched down next to the prone little filly with the big white blaze on her face that she'd watched running in the pasture just days ago. Her eyes were closed and Shannon couldn't see her rib cage moving.

Oh, God, was the filly dead?

Next to her, lying in the straw, was a small, disposable syringe with a bent needle. And beside that was a small brown glass bottle. It was empty.

Dear God, it couldn't be!

Fisting her hands to her mouth, Shannon was finally able to move and pushed her way into the stall, crouching down next to Tim, who said gruffly, after checking her breathing, "She's alive, but just barely." Then he yanked his phone out of his back pocket and was relaying the emergency to Sean's vet seconds later.

"Who would do such a thing?" Shannon whispered. Then she pointed with a shaky finger to the bottle with no label. "And what is that?"

Tim looked up from the filly, his eyes ripe with sadness. "I'm not sure, but I know what it sure looks like."

Don't say it. Don't make it true.

Shannon heard a commotion from the other end of the barn and then, "Where is everybody?" It was Sean.

Tim's mouth was set in a grim line when he stood up and called out, waving Sean over. "We're down here, Muldoon. Hurry."

In seconds, Sean's head appeared above the stall. He took one look at what they were crouched next to and began spewing rapid Gaelic, frowning darkly. What he was saying needed no translation. It was clear he was cursing. Then he was in the stall next to Shannon, hunkered down with the glass bottle in his hand. Bringing it to his nose, he took a cautious sniff and swore again.

Tim said in a reassuring tone, "Rick's on his way and will be here in just a minute. Luckily, he's with the yearlings doing routine physicals."

"When did you find her?" Sean asked quietly.

She glanced slowly between the men and the unnaturally still filly as the ramifications of what she was witnessing hit her. Her body went tight as a cinched corset and her brain began to shut down all functionality. She was very close to having a completely dissociated panic attack. She could feel it closing over her, trapping her, and it filled her with pain. Blinking rapidly, her breath came in fast, shallow bursts as her body began to shake and her mind screamed denial. She viciously wanted to continue believing this new version of events she'd created where Sean wasn't really drugging his horses and was instead innocent and good. She wasn't so sure her heart could handle it being any other way.

Just then the vet came racing into the barn carrying a medical bag. "I'm here. Where is she?"

Shannon jerked away from Sean and stood up, pointing at the unconscious filly. "We found her a few minutes ago. What is the stuff, Sean? What did somebody inject her with?" *Tell me it wasn't steroids. Please.*

Sean took another sniff of the bottle, his green eyes flat and devoid of emotion when he replied. "I don't know, exactly." But she could tell by the way his jaw clenched that he had his suspicions.

"It looks like somebody drugged your foal," Tim stated without pretense.

Sean's gaze whipped up to him and then to Shannon. "Obviously."

Trembling, Shannon started to back out of the stall. The brown bottle he was holding was the same size around as the dust mark left in the medicine locker she'd seen, and it made her want to weep. Just when she'd been so sure of his innocence.

This changed everything.

Now she didn't know what to think. So she didn't. Couldn't if she tried.

Instead she just walked away.

Chapter Fifteen

"SHANNON, WAIT!" SEAN called after her. Her face had gone pale and her eyes huge with dilated pupils before she'd spun around and sprinted out of the barn. With his heart beating a punishing rhythm and feeling heartsick over his foal, he rose to his feet, intent on following her.

But he was stopped when Tim said quietly, "We've got a real problem, Sean."

Like he didn't already know. His gut had gone raw and slippery. "I know." In his heart he knew—and it scared the piss out of him.

Mickey O'Banion.

It was the only explanation. He and his boys were the only ones with real motivation to go after Zeke or one of his foals, because they were the only ones who knew the stallion's real secret—his true identity. Even though his coat had changed from bay to gray as he'd matured and he had no white markings, Sean had obviously been naïve in believing that the change was enough to keep his identity hidden forever. When he'd first agreed to accept the bet that night at Flannery's, he'd learned of Zeke's lineage, how his great-grandsire was the legendary Shergar. In fact, it was O'Banion's men who'd originally stolen Shergar at gunpoint and hidden him away.

The mob boss hadn't been kidding when he'd said his new foal came from the finest stud farm in the country—Mickey's own.

"Do you think it's an inside job?" Tim asked, his voice colored with worry.

He shook his head. "It's not."

"How can you be so sure of that?" The trainer lifted his cowboy hat and scratched at an itch near his hairline. "It'd be easy enough for one of the stable hands to do it."

He clenched his jaw. "It's not them," he ground out, growing irritated.

Tim stared at him unblinking for long seconds. Finally he said, "Then it's the competition—another breeder, a rival farm."

Callum Charlemagne came instantly to mind. But Sean dismissed that suspicion. Mostly. On the off chance that it wasn't the Irish mob that'd done this, he'd be foolish to rule out that old bastard. He'd hated Sean since the beginning.

Sean nodded once—just once. "Yes. That's most likely it."

"You want me to call the police?"

He shook his head, knowing he should be the one to do it. "I'll phone the guards." He figured having his property crawling with the law would keep anyone unsavory at bay for a while. Long enough to figure out a plan at least, hopefully.

With one last glance at the foal who'd shown such spunk and promise just yesterday, his heart bruised and aching, Sean made his way out of the stall. "Leave everything as it is, Tim. Don't touch anything. We want to give the authorities as much to go on as possible."

Out of the corner of his eye, he saw Tim frown. "That might be a problem then. Shannon touched everything."

Christ. The last thing he needed was for her to wind up a bloody suspect. "Well, then you can explain that when they get here."

Leaving Tim, Sean strode out of the barn into the bright Rocky Mountain sunshine. Squinting against the sun, he pulled his cell phone from the front pocket of his jeans, looked up the number, and dialed the Fortune police. The line had just picked up and a female dispatch answered when he saw Shannon slip into the trees that separated his house from the barns. Where in the bloody world was she going?

But before he could go find out, he was distracted by having to answer a ton of questions. When the dispatcher had all the information she needed, he hung up and prepared to be bombarded by the police.

Lovely.

Still, as much as he hated it and as uncomfortable as it made him, this was his responsibility. If someone else besides O'Banion really was behind the attacks, then he needed to know. Because he wanted a bloody clear conscience just once in his life when he lay his head down on his pillow at night. Waking up in cold sweats at three a.m. had become his nightly routine, and it was getting really old. When he'd fled Ireland for a new life, it hadn't occurred to him how draining it would be to spend the rest of his life always looking over his shoulder, waiting for the other shoe to drop.

Or just how much he'd have to sacrifice.

"Hey, Sean!" came a shout from behind him. Turning his head, he spotted his stable hand Stew coming toward him. The guy was pure Texan with his handlebar mustache and ten-gallon hat. He had an awful habit of chewing, but was magic with the horses. "I just came back from a ride on the front forty, and ya ain't gonna like what I seen."

There was more? Could the day get any worse? "What's out there?"

The wiry horseman stopped a few feet away and hooked his thumb over his shoulder back in the direction of the highway. "There's a news reporter set up down at the gate. When he saw me, the reporter started asking me some mighty pushy questions about Something Unexpected's injury at Belmont, so I told 'em I didn't know what the devil he was yammerin' on about. I told him he was plum crazy."

Why was a reporter sniffing around about Zeke's injury? Just what he needed. Christ. What a goddamn mess.

Scrubbing a hand over his face, Sean inhaled deeply and said, "Thanks for the heads-up, Stew. Why don't ye go on and check on Zeke—maybe stay with him for a while. He was acting surly earlier, and I think he's feeling pent up and restless. He could use the company."

There was also the added benefit that having someone sitting with him would make him less vulnerable.

The Texan nodded briskly. "Ya got it, boss."

Just then the distinctive sound of wheels on gravel permeated the air and he closed his eyes, took a deep breath. He could do this. He could give the guards a statement and show them the crime scene. And he could keep it together.

Nobody had to know that inside he was shaking.

HE'D MADE IT. He'd survived.

Those were Sean's only thoughts as he watched the last squad car pull out and head down his driveway early that evening, the sky overhead dark and foreboding with an impending storm. Thunder threatened in the distance. When had that come in? It'd been nothing but clear skies an hour ago.

He shrugged. Such was weather in Colorado.

Before anything else could stop him, he went to find Shannon. It had been hours since she'd run out of the barn and he was worried about her. Her eyes had looked so dark and anguished.

Sean stepped onto his front porch as the sky opened up and started dumping rain, but he wasn't prepared for his screen door to swing open with a screech as Shannon came out, her arms crossed and her eyes puffy. It was obvious she'd been crying. Christ, he'd been afraid of that. And he'd been worried about it for the past hour.

Before he could stop himself, he reached out and yanked her to him, hugging her hard. The instant his body came into contact with hers, she started shaking. "Hey now, *a mhuirnin*," he whispered softly.

For a long moment, she hugged him back, her head against his chest and her fingers curled into his back. But then she was shoving away, demanding, "Tell me it's not true."

He searched her gaze, confused. "What are you talking about? The filly isn't going to die, if that's what you're asking, Shannon. She'll live, thankfully."

She raked a hand through her hair, turned to walk away, then came back to him, eyes dark and wounded-looking. Stopping in front of him, she tilted her head and said, "Was it a drug overdose?"

"It appears it was, yes." He nodded.

She exploded. "Why, Sean? Why the hell are you pumping your horses full of steroids? Is winning that big of a deal?"

Shock froze him in place and he stammered, dumbfounded at the accusation. "You—you think I did this? That I'm doping me runners?"

"I do." She had her arms crossed tightly and nodded curtly, her lips pressed in a tight line.

"What kind of piece of shite feck do you take me for, Shannon?" How could she even ask such a thing?

"I don't know, Sean. You tell me."

"Tell me what you're doing in my house, first," he countered, feeling defensive. He wasn't the type of arsehole who'd shoot up his horses just to win a few races.

Aside from the fact that postrace drug testing was mandatory and hiding that sort of abuse would be incredibly hard, he simply wouldn't do that. Bottom line. And he was suddenly starting to get pissed that she thought so little of him.

Spinning on her heels, she threw her nose in the air and disappeared inside his home just like she owned the place herself. If he weren't so offended at the moment over her accusations, it would have warmed his heart to see the woman he was mad for treat his home with such familiarity. As it was, it just drove him batty.

He followed her inside and let the screen door shut with a resounding slap. "Well?" He growled after her. "What's your bloody reason?"

She stopped in front of the living room fireplace but rounded when he neared. "I couldn't be in *that* building, okay? I needed somewhere else to be," she suddenly shouted, her hands fisting at her sides. Shannon's eyes turned on him, round as saucers and swimming with emotion. "She was just a baby." Her voice broke on a sob.

Something inside him responded to her anguish and he went to her, pulled by an irresistible need to give her comfort. "Hush now. The vet is doing everything he can. With a little luck she'll be right as rain very soon." And he wrapped her up in his arms again. She was still shaking and his heart broke a little. Today's travesty had been really hard on her. For many long moments he simply held her to him, giving and receiving comfort. Slowly, her fists unfurled against him, her fingers digging gently into his lower back. Then her breathing slowed and became steady. "That's it," he crooned softly against her hair before inhaling the lemon scent of her shampoo.

Yearning reared up inside him, swift and strong. Christ, he wanted this woman in his life. He couldn't have her, but he bloody well wanted her anyway. Even if only once. Because he'd begun to realize something. Something profound.

His heart had chosen Shannon.

He didn't want to die without knowing what it was like to be with her, selfish as that might be. This whole time he'd been keeping her at arms' length thinking it was in her best interest. But was it really?

Shannon shifted and mumbled something against his chest that he couldn't understand. Pulling back, Sean asked gently, "What was that you said, love?"

Lifting her head, she met his gaze with her gorgeous brown eyes and his chest went tight, making him wheeze slightly. "I said that I needed to know the truth."

Still short on breath, he was a little surprised that he managed, "What truth?"

Her big brown eyes bore into him, branding his soul. "Are you using steroids on your horses?"

"I'm not," he said softly, definitively.

For what seemed like forever, but was probably only a few seconds, she simply stared at him in silence. Then she must have decided something because her shoulders slumped and she curled into him, tucking her head under his chin.

"I shouldn't believe you," she whispered.

"Why not?" It was a real question. What reason did she have not to believe him? Well, other than the fact that she'd found a used needle and empty bottle with the injured foal. That looked suspect, he had to admit.

"I have my reasons."

"Don't we all?" He murmured into her hair.

"Mine are really good."

That got a chuckle out of him. "Want to share?"

She shook her head against his chest, her silky hair rubbing against him with the movement. "Nu-uh."

"You certain?" he replied almost absently as his body began to stir with desire. The way her breasts were pushing against him was slowly starting to drive him crazy.

"I don't want to share," she said, her voice sounding a little breathy. "I want to do something else."

Before he could respond, she lifted onto her toes and did something completely unexpected—and totally arousing.

She kissed him. Hard. And in that instant, Sean made a life-altering decision.

Tonight, Shannon was his.

Chapter Sixteen

ABANDONING CAUTION, SHANNON surrendered to her feelings. The way Sean's demanding mouth moved over hers made it impossible to do anything else. There was such a raw honesty in the way he kissed her, the way he held her. It touched her very core. Good God, how she wanted this man.

Like nothing she'd ever wanted before.

A tide of emotion crashed over her, and Shannon dug her fingers into his back, riding a wave of need. Heat poured like molten gold into the pit of her belly, and she pushed against him, the sudden sensitivity between her legs begging for his touch. He responded with a throaty groan and grabbed her ass with his large, work-hardened hands and pulled her full against him, grinding slowly.

With an equally slow and arousing tug of her bottom lip, he pulled away to whisper in a voice gone rough and unsteady, "I've got to be with you. I can't wait anymore."

He trailed his lips along her jaw, making her shiver with desire, until he reached her ear and whispered darkly, "Let me have you."

Yes, please.

Though the small part of her that was still functioning rationally knew this was a mistake for several reasons—all of them legitimate and practical and sound—it didn't matter. None of it mattered compared to how much her heart wanted this—wanted *him*.

Letting go, Shannon slid her hands down his back and around his lean, corded waist, reveling in all his rock-hard muscles. There were benefits to boxing. His body was sculpted and defined and so, so toned. And yet, when she slipped her fingers under the edge of his T-shirt, she discovered his skin was velvet soft to the touch.

"Oh, Shannon." He breathed, his stomach muscles flexing under her fingertips. When she reached the front button of his jeans, she grabbed it and tugged gently, teasing. Though she really wasn't. She was wet and achy and wanted every impressive inch of what she felt bulging beneath his fly.

Shannon cried out in surprise when Sean moved suddenly, his tough hands gripping the back of her thighs and lifting her up, wrapping them around his waist. And then he was striding across the hardwood floor, his boots thumping loudly while he found her nipple with his mouth and tongued it through the fabric of her shirt. The friction caused by his tongue on the thin cotton had her swollen and ready before they made it to his bedroom down the hall.

His lips closed around her and he sucked hard enough to make her gasp in surprise at the surge of heat it sent straight to her pussy. "Sean!" she cried out, impatient now for him to be naked so she could touch him, hold his hot, thick cock in her hands. "Clothes off," she demanded between pants of mounting need. "Take them off."

But before he did, a flash of lightning split the sky. It lit the room just as Sean looked up, a wicked glint in his amazing eyes. "Ladies first." And he kissed her again, slow and drugging, his tongue mating with hers in a lazy, sensual rhythm that had her melting boneless onto the comforter when he lowered her still clothed to the bed. "I've been dreaming about you," he whispered hotly against her lips and thrust against her, rubbing gently.

Moaning in pleasure, Shannon tightened her legs around his waist, using her feet to pull him even closer, loving the delicious pressure of his erection pushing into her. "Oh, yeah?" she whispered back, enticed. "What kind of dreams?"

He ducked his head and found the base of her neck, biting playfully. "Naughty, naked kinds of dreams."

Shannon laughed. "Is that so?"

Now he was skimming his firm, sculpted lips along her collarbone as his hands gripped both of hers, pinning them against the bed. Sean rocked his hard-on against her, holding the pressure there until they were both panting unsteadily. "Want details?" he said with enough heat in his voice that she wasn't sure if he was joking.

The thought of him describing his sex dreams to her was deeply arousing. It had her so swollen and throbbing and slick that she tremored slightly, a tightening inside her pussy like the beginning of an orgasm. Delicious. "*Mmm*," she moaned, smiling. "Yes, please."

He went still, swearing. Then he moved swiftly in the dim room, stripping Shannon naked. Sean's hands roamed up her legs possessively, impatiently, after he'd completed the task. "I'd rather show you," he growled, the edgy sound of it making her shiver with need.

When he reached her center, he skimmed a finger over the curls at her opening, teasing the sensitive, slick fold. "Christ, you're so wet for me. I can already feel you." He looked up and pinned her with a stare, his eyes like emerald fire. "I need to taste you."

Shannon's head fell back against the soft comforter, and her legs spread easily for him. Having his mouth on her was everything she wanted. Everything she could need. Sean made her burn and ache and feel so many emotions that she couldn't sort one out from another. All she knew was that being with him this way now was no longer as simple as a choice being made. It was a need that rose from someplace deep inside her that had been locked and buried and forgotten for years as she'd placed everyone else's needs in front of her own.

Raking her hands through his black hair and fisting there just as his tongue replaced his finger and he stroked over her slowly, leisurely—like her pussy was an ice cream cone and she his favorite flavor. Good God, the man could please. Gasping, floating on a sea of desire,

Shannon spread her legs wider and pulled up her knees until her feet were flat on the bed and she was arching wantonly into him.

"Sean." She breathed, dazed with passion. "Oh. My. God." And that was the last of her coherent speech, because he'd found her clit and began licking her, kissing her hotly.

Rain pounded steady against the windows, the sound like perfectly planned mood music as Shannon let herself go. Soon her eyes were closed, her head rolling back and forth as she moaned and Sean spoke to her darkly, erotically—urging her to come. His voice had gone rough and his accent heavy. And when he started coaxing her to orgasm and slipped into Gaelic, murmuring words she couldn't understand but that sounded so incredibly sexy, Shannon arched into him one last time and cried out, orgasming almost violently. It ripped through her hard and fast, leaving her weak.

"Oh, you don't think I'm done, do you?" Sean said, but his voice sounded far away from where Shannon was currently floating.

Then he was stripping off his own clothes and standing at the foot of the bed naked, breathing hard, his thick, gorgeous cock heavy with arousal. Shannon's body reacted to the sight instantly, surprising her. Multiple orgasms had never been her body's thing. But by the way her pussy was growing hot and throbbing again, she knew that another one was building.

Because of Sean.

The man had the most amazing body. So hard and tough from his years of boxing, his arms and abs were ripped and sculpted perfectly. The slight dusting of chest hair and happy trail that ended in a thatch of curly black hair nestled around his erection only served to remind Shannon that he was an all masculine, virile male.

Before she could stop herself, she rose onto her knees and went to him, crawling naked toward him over the bed sheets. Her skin was prickly and hot and almost too tight, desire building hard and fast again inside her. The only thing that would appease it would be his hands all over her. She needed them on every square inch of inflamed skin.

But first it was her turn to do the tasting.

"What are you doing, love?" Sean asked softly, his gorgeous eyelashes lowered over his passion-filled gaze. His heavy, sculpted thighs were braced apart and she ran her hands up them, scraping her nails along his skin gently. She smiled when he sucked in deep. Finally her hands reached him and she thrilled at his quick intake of breath and the way he hissed through his teeth.

"This," she replied and placed her mouth around him, flicking the plump head of his cock with her tongue. No one had ever inspired her to want to do this before, but Sean made her feel things, made her *want* things. And right now she wanted him in her mouth.

Sean swore violently as she took him deep and rocked toward her, his hands fisting in her loose hair. "Feck. Jesus, Shannon."

Smiling around him, feeling wild and adventurous, she took her time sucking and exploring the velvet steel length of him until he was panting heavily. Glorying in her newfound sexuality, she laughed when he grabbed her by the shoulders and pushed her away a little roughly. "Too much for you, baby?" she teased, amazed at herself. Who was this woman?

But before she could begin to feel embarrassed and pull out of the moment, Sean had covered himself with protection and was on her, stretching out his big, hard body over her. The thick head of his cock split her folds and she moaned in anticipation. And when he pushed into her with one hard thrust, she cried out at the sensation of such incredible fullness.

"Shannon," he groaned, like the sound had been ripped from his chest. For a suspended moment he was still. But then her inner muscles tightened around him involuntarily and Sean dropped his forehead to hers as he began thrusting slow and deep and steady. "You're exquisite," he whispered against her lips.

And she felt that way. With every single thrust of his hips, every caress of his hand, every heated, passionate look he gave her, she felt exquisite—and beautiful and wanted and free.

"Come for me," he suddenly demanded, his movements becoming faster, harder. She could feel him on the brink. And knowing that created a rush of desire so intense that she had no choice but to obey. And when she came this time he was right there with her, groaning, thrusting one last time with his own release—the most incredible orgasm of her life taking her over.

SEAN LISTENED TO the rain pound against the windows as Shannon dozed quietly next to him, her body half flung over his. He was gently skimming his fingers over her, enjoying the silky feel of her skin, and his brain was blank as feck because he couldn't think after what had just happened.

Shannon had blown his mind.

"What do I do now?" he whispered almost silently, his gaze directed up toward the ceiling. Whether he was asking God or Jesus or somebody for help, he didn't know. All he knew was that his feelings for Shannon were scary strong, and he was in over his head.

Now that he'd had her, there was no way he was going to be able to stop. And while one part of him—the part that had just been fucked senseless by the woman of his dreams—was already looking forward to round two, the other part remembered all too well who Sean Connor Donaghy really was and knew he had just made a huge mistake.

But then Shannon moved against him, snuggling closer, and he just didn't have the heart to shut it down and walk away. Not when everything he'd ever wanted was lying right there in his arms. Not when he'd given up the hope of ever getting so lucky.

But most especially, not when he'd just fallen in love.

Chapter Seventeen

THREE DAYS LATER, Shannon was at the Hole in The Wall bakery sitting across from her sister again. Three wonderful, amazing days filled with Sean and a whole lot of really, really great sex.

And it must have shown all over her face.

"You slut!" Colleen shot her a wicked grin. "You slept with him."

There was no point in denying it. "Of course I have," Shannon replied nonchalantly, like sleeping with Sean was the most natural, evolutionary step in the world. Which it actually had been, oddly. Doubts and fears aside, making love with Sean really had been the most natural thing she'd ever done. Maybe not the wisest, but it sure was easy.

And fun. Wow, was it fun.

Colleen huffed and tore off a piece of glazed donut, shoving it in her mouth. "I can tell it was good. You're glowing," she said as she chewed. Very unladylike. No one would ever guess in a million years that she came from one of the most prestigious families in America. The woman ate like a trucker. "Even though I'm shamelessly jealous and hate you a little bit right now, I want details."

Shannon snorted and looked out the front window at the people passing by. "Not in a million years." How could she explain something she couldn't even wrap her own mind around because her heart kept getting in the way?

"Is he hung?" her sister asked after she'd taken a big swig of straight black coffee. "I bet he's hung."

Shannon glared, feeling embarrassed. "That's none of your business." *But yes, yes he was.*

"Oh, come on, Shan. It's been too long for me and I'm feeling desperate. Give me something to live vicariously by." Colleen looked sincerely put out, presumably by the fact that she hadn't had sex in what, maybe six months? Shannon really doubted it'd been longer than that for her sister, not with her "sex with someone new at least twice a year" rule.

Shannon did some quick mental math, realizing just how many partners that would be if she herself had held fast to that rule. Colleen was doing laps around her. Not that it would be hard to do, given that Sean made partner number three.

Hey, the third time was supposed to be charmed, right? Shannon's stomach quivered excitedly at the idea. *Sweet.*

Wouldn't that be lucky?

Colleen was staring at her expectantly, so Shannon caved a little and gave her something. "He knows what he's doing with the female anatomy."

A pale blond eyebrow lifted. *"Really?"* And then, "That's all you're going to tell me? That he's good with pussies?" She leaned back in her seat, crossed her arms, and glared. "Like that wasn't already obvious."

Shannon tipped her head to one side. "I didn't realize you wanted a detailed summary of my sex life. Although, judging by the way you keep scanning the place, I'm beginning to think you asked to meet here hoping for another glimpse of something—or *somebody*—of your own." She ended with a wink.

Her sister sighed, deep and weary. "Okay, it's true."

"What's true?" Shannon said, really looking at her sister. There were dark smudges under her hazel eyes and her coloring was paler than normal under her freckles, like she hadn't been getting enough sleep. "What's going on?" Suddenly her good mood went south as she became swamped with worry.

Colleen tossed her blond hair over her shoulder and held up a hand, her index and middle finger in a V. "Two things."

"Okay," Shannon drawled.

"The first thing is, yes, you're right. I have been scoping the place. That guy we saw last time we were here has been stuck in my head and I can't get him out. You know—Mr. Badass? A big part of me was hoping I'd see him while I was here to tell you the second thing, and if he's single, I planned on climbing him like a mountain and howling from his peak like a coyote."

Now that was a visual.

But before Shannon could laugh, Colleen continued, "But the real reason I asked you to meet me is that I found something. And before you say anything, yes, I have been doing research—not just frolicking about in Fortune having a grand time. You're involved in something, so it's important."

"Thank you," Shannon said, and watched as Apple and a small group of women walked by, talking excitedly. When her new friend looked up and saw her, the blond waved with a big friendly smile. "I'll believe you if you say you found something on Dad. But it's difficult to believe that you could have found anything on Sean."

"Why, because you slept with him?" Colleen eyed her seriously. "You do realize that sex doesn't automatically make him innocent, right?"

Well, yeah. She'd decided on his innocence *before* having sex with him. Big difference. "I know that, Colleen. What did you find?" she asked, hoping to move the conversation away from her and Sean's bedroom activities.

Colleen pulled a plain tan file folder from her bag and handed it across the booth to Shannon. "I think I've found something significant. I'm not positive, but I've got that buzzy feeling. It all began with a Google search on the word *O'Banion*. That alone didn't herald anything noteworthy, so I added the words 'horseracing' and 'gambling' into the search engine with it. This is what I discovered."

Taking the file from her hands, Shannon opened it and set it on the table. She glanced up at her sister. "Explain to me what I'm seeing."

Colleen leaned forward and tapped a photocopied picture of a racehorse running full out, its jockey leaned far over its neck as they flew down the track. "Okay, I'll walk you through. That's Something Unexpected, Sean's horse. Notice the tongue hanging out of the corner of his mouth?"

She nodded and said, "I do. I've seen video clips of him and noticed he has that quirk when he's running."

Her sister flipped the paper over, revealing the next one below. It was another racehorse running on the track, its tongue lolling out of the side of its mouth too. Only this horse was bay and the photo looked old. "This is that famous Irish racehorse, Shergar," her sister said. "Remember that story?"

Shannon nodded, her eyes squinting on the photo. Picking it up, she held it next to the photo of Zeke. "I'll be damned," she mumbled. "I wonder if Tim was right."

"Who's Tim?"

Blinking, she laid the photos back down and explained. "He's Sean's yearling trainer. I was talking to him a few days ago and he mentioned to me that it's rumored that Zeke was descended from Shergar. But that doesn't make sense because that horse disappeared in the early eighties. His bloodline died with him."

Her sister tapped the picture of Zeke. "Did it? During my research, I ran across a lot of articles related to Shergar's story. The official report is that the Irish mob abducted him. But there are a dozen theories surrounding his abduction and what really happened to him. They range from him being ransomed by the Irish Republican Army in an arms deal to being kidnapped by Libyan extremists. And one of the theories is that he didn't actually die, that he was kidnapped and became a prized stud at a secret breeding operation in Northern Ireland, where he lived well into old age and sired many offspring that were sold for a fortune to wealthy people around the world." She tapped the picture again. "Look at his tongue, Shannon. Shergar was famous for that move. What if Zeke really is Shergar's grandson?"

She saw the ramifications. "It would make him priceless. But I don't get what that has to do with Dad, though, or O'Banion."

Her sister leaned back and picked up her coffee, sipping. "You should look at the other pages."

She did. One was an *Irish Times* newspaper article about a man named Mickey O'Banion who was indicted in connection with the mob over an illegal horseracing betting ring but later cleared when they failed to find substantial evidence against him.

Chills ran down her spine. "You think that's the same O'Banion that Dad owes money to?"

"I think it might be," Colleen replied after hesitating briefly. "Though to be fair, that article was written almost twenty years ago. Still, I think there's a connection."

Looking at the pictures of the horses and their matching lolling tongues, Shannon had to agree even though she didn't like it. "Thanks for sharing this. I need to sit on it for a while, but I'm sure you're right."

It was hard as hell believing that their dad was neck deep in something probably highly illegal—maybe even dangerous. "What do we do if this turns out to be really bad?" she asked, voicing her biggest fear. "What if he's got me involved in all of this?" She waved her hand over the open file folder.

"Then we hop the first plane we can catch and leave the country. I hear Cuba's finally back on the tourist map," Colleen said with a sparkle in her eye, clearly trying to lighten the mood.

Tipping her head, Shannon decided to play along. "Mmm, I'm more a cool weather fan. How's Norway sound?"

"Only if you promise to change your clothes. You've been wearing the same ones for weeks. It's embarrassing."

Shannon took offense. "Hey, they're clean. I wash them regularly." Buying more had fallen so far off her radar with everything that had been happening, she was a little embarrassed. Normally she was well versed in the ways of clothing rotation.

Just then the bell over the door chimed and Colleen whipped her head around. But it wasn't the guy. It was just a young couple with a baby in a front carrier. Shannon tried not to laugh at the look of disappointment on her sister's face. "Sorry, hon."

"Me too."

They fell into silence, Shannon drinking her coffee and Colleen pouting into hers. Shannon took some time to study the old-fashioned bakery with its homey smells and faded yellow walls covered in black-and-white photos while she sifted through this new information. If this O'Banion guy was the same one that their father was indebted to, then that would mean their dad was in bed with the mob, which sucked. And made her more than a little scared. But she still didn't see what the Irish mob would have to do with Sean and his horse.

Maybe the best thing for her to do was to talk with Tim again. "I'm going to ask Sean's trainer. See if I can get any more information from him. And you should snoop in Dad's office too when you get back to Saratoga, to see if anything new turns up." She had a thought. "Oh, and you should check in with Mom. You know how she gets to rambling when she's had too many Xanax. You might be able to get something useful from her."

Colleen gave a quick nod. "Will do. And I'll let you know the moment I find anything, if I do."

She agreed. "Yeah, we'll keep each other posted."

That seemed to conclude things, so Shannon thought on something else, knowing that everything she'd just learned would sift in the background of her mind and fall into place if she just relaxed a bit. "Hey, in all seriousness, do you ever wonder what it would be like to drop everything and just start a new life somewhere else—somewhere like here?" Shannon asked suddenly, thinking of Sean, but also thinking of herself. There was this tiny burning speck of desire inside her to do that very thing.

And it was growing.

Colleen surprised her. "All the fucking time."

Shannon sighed, feeling torn. On the one hand, she loved her family. But on the other, she'd never gotten what she really wanted or needed from them, or her life back east. After all of this was said and done, was that what she was going to go back to?

And could she?

Struggling against a sudden surge of panic, she shifted restlessly. "Then why do we do it, Leenie? Why am I here?"

"Because you're loyal, Shannon. That's why. And because you have the biggest, softest heart of anyone I know."

That didn't help. "I think it's because I let him treat me like a doormat. I think it's because deep down I'm too much of a coward to stand up to Mom and Dad."

Colleen didn't even blink. "Then stop being one."

"How?" She really didn't know. How did someone stand up to family without just coming off like a selfish jerk?

"You tell me." And that's when her sister smiled with such unexpected self-loathing it was jarring.

Shannon sighed, her body shaking from nerves. "We're a pair, aren't we?"

The bell over the door jingled again, signaling a new customer. Shannon didn't even need to look over her shoulder to know it was him—*the guy*. She knew it because her sister's eyes went wide and excited like a kid on Christmas.

"It's *him*." The way Colleen said it made it sound like he was some mythical being that only showed himself to the worthy. It made her laugh. And it helped ease her anxiety back to a manageable level. Thank God.

"What are you going to do?" Shannon asked as The Guy began making his way through the booths to the back counter. This time he was wearing a white T-shirt with a picture of Ron Swanson from *Parks and Recreation* on the front with the slogan "Be a Man." Though he didn't appear to be having any problems in that department. Heck, no.

Colleen blurted out, "I love him!" So loud that the guy stopped halfway through the bakery and pinned her with some seriously gorgeous baby blues.

Shannon couldn't believe it; Colleen's face went bright red with embarrassment. And there she was thinking her sister was immune to such feelings.

"Ron Swanson," she stammered to explain under his intense scrutiny. "Not you."

The Guy looked at her sister and gave her a very thorough sizing-up, from her flip-flop covered feet to the top of her pale blond hair, not missing the tank top and shorts in between. When he was done, his gaze came back to meet hers and a slow smile spread across his face. "Give me an hour and you'll change your mind about who you love, sweet thing."

Colleen almost fell out of her seat. "Promise?" she said, clearly hoping to make him laugh.

But before they could flirt any more, a plump woman in her early sixties stepped out from the back hallway and waved to him. With what appeared to be some regret, The Guy gave her sister a wink and said in a voice as rough as the rest of him, "When you're ready to know, you come find me."

Completely disregarding everyone else in the bakery who was listening, Colleen called after him, "Where do I find you?"

"Ask Stone. He'll know."

And then the badass with the tattoos and a smile hot enough to vaporize Colleen's panties strode through the back archway and out of sight. Whipping back around, she looked at Shannon with big round eyes. "Do you think he was kidding?"

"He doesn't look like the kind of guy who jokes about that sort of thing," Shannon replied honestly.

Colleen nodded. "Good. That's what I was hoping."

Narrowing her eyes on her sister, Shannon asked, "What are you planning?"

Colleen couldn't even try looking innocent. The girl just ended up looking like a cat who'd swallowed the canary. "Nothing."

Right. And Shannon wasn't planning on getting Sean naked as soon as she saw him again, either. "Fine. Just remember to be careful. Use protection."

Waving her off, Colleen replied, "Always." Then her expression went serious and she said, "Now that that's settled, let's get back to your problems."

Let's not, shall we?

But Shannon just sighed, knowing it was for the best.

"Hey, wait a minute," Colleen said, breaking into her gloomy thoughts. "Who's Stone?"

Shannon smirked. "Wouldn't you like to know?"

Her sister nodded earnestly. "Yes, yes I would."

Taking the opportunity to torment her, she grabbed her purse and stood from the booth, preparing to leave. "It's too bad that I'm suddenly in a rush and have to go. Sorry."

"You wouldn't," Colleen replied, her eyes narrowed in disbelief. "You know my time here is up and I have to fly back to Saratoga tonight. Help a woman out, will you?"

Shannon just shrugged her shoulders delicately. "I've got places to go, things to do."

"Well, I've got some*one* to do before I go, Shannon—so damn it, don't cop out on me." Colleen grabbed her things and scrambled from the booth after her.

But she was already pushing the door open with a jingle of the bell, laughter trailing behind her as she stepped out into the bright Colorado sunshine. "We'll catch up soon. Gotta go, love you!"

"Who's Stone?"

She pulled her sunglasses from her purse and put them on. My, it was a lovely day.

"Shannon?"

And the sky? Oh, it was *such* a gorgeous shade of blue. "*Shannon!*"

Laughter broke loose, but she just kept on walking, knowing it was killing Colleen. God, she loved her sister. She was so easy to tease. Handily, it also kept her from obsessing about her own reality.

At the moment, that's exactly what she needed.

She'd expected her sister to follow, but when she turned around at the end of the block, Colleen was nowhere to be found. Shrugging her shoulders, she waited for a car to pass and crossed the street, the new information swirling around in her head. What did it all mean?

Pondering it, Shannon didn't notice how far she had walked until she came to a crowd gathered in the small grassy park at the end of Main Street. Moving closer, she took in the balloons, music, and the sound of happy dogs barking. What was going on?

Shannon had just stepped onto the grass under a shady oak tree when the music cut out and she heard someone speak from a microphone, the sound loud and echoing. "Step right up, everyone, and get your picture taken with the Bachelors of Fortune. You know you want to."

What?

Moving forward more quickly, Shannon was trying to poke her way through the crowd to get a better look when Apple sauntered up next to her, grinning like crazy. "I can't believe the guys are doing this. It's so great. I've already had my picture taken."

Pushing her hair over her shoulder, Shannon looked at Apple, noting she was wearing another vintage style dress and sandals. "What's going on?" Just then she caught the faint whiff of popcorn and felt even more confused. "Why does it feel like a carnival around here—only without the Ferris wheel and Zipper?"

Apple laughed, her big blue eyes dancing. "Why, because it's Fortune's annual Pet Adoption Day! Every summer the local animal shelter hosts this big charity event and brings in all kinds of family-friendly activities, like the bouncy houses over there and the cake walk and face painting. People are invited to support the shelter by buying tickets to the games or simply by adopting one of the animals. And this year the shelter director, Marcia Boone, got the Bachelors of Fortune to come sign autographs and take pictures with the locals."

Could that be any sweeter?

At that moment the tall, balding man who'd been standing directly in front of her shifted and she got a clear view of things. Sean was standing next to Aidan and Jake, and the three of them were having their picture taken with a plump, middle-aged woman and a small, shaking Chihuahua. After the photographer finished, the woman turned to Jake and gave him a smacking kiss on the cheek. "You guys are adorable!"

She couldn't agree more. Especially when the next person in line handed Sean her new family member to pose with—a fluffy black and white bunny rabbit—and he simply smiled and scratched it between its big floppy ears. When the photo op was over, he handed it back to the young girl and noticed Shannon through the crowd.

The heat in his smile cranked up about a thousand degrees. And her heart flopped right on over in her chest.

"So how are things progressing with Jake?" she asked Apple, hoping for a distraction. Because right then, all she wanted to do was get Sean alone and show him everything she was feeling. Which was a lot. A *lot*.

Apple waved a hand dismissively. "Oh, you know, it's not. Not really. That man is the most obstinate, tight-lipped person you'll ever meet. It's going to take just the right thing to crack him." She glanced over at Shannon. "I've got something I'm working on. Don't you worry."

A woman Shannon didn't know called out to Apple, beckoning her over.

"Duty calls," the blond said with an apologetic smile. "We'll talk again soon?"

"Of course," Shannon said and gave her friend a quick hug. "Do your thing."

Which left Shannon once again alone to watch the Bachelors of Fortune pose and sign autographs like real celebrities. Sure, part of her wanted to go talk to Sean, but another part of her was really enjoying hanging back and observing him in action. The man was just so darned *nice*.

Someone stepped up beside her then, turning her attention. It was a short, homely man with dark eyes and a nose that was so misshapen it almost looked like a blob of Play-Doh had been molded onto his face. Just the sight of it made her own nose twitch in sympathy. Whatever had happened to him, it must have hurt like crazy.

"Beautiful day, ain't it?" he said in a thick Irish accent.

Suddenly uneasy but not knowing why, she nodded and agreed. "Yes, it is." She kept her gaze locked on Sean through the crowd. He was busy talking to a group of Boy Scouts, his hands gesturing animatedly.

"How's your father these days?" the man asked unexpectedly.

Startled, she whipped her gaze to him, and demanded, "How do you know my father?"

The man laughed, the sound hollow and creepy. "Because it's my job to know. Tell him that I'm watching."

What did that mean?

Before she could ask him, he melted into the crowd, and Shannon was left feeling confused and alone in a sea of people.

Holy crap, what was happening?

Chapter Eighteen

LATER THAT DAY, Sean stepped into the office doorway as Shannon glanced up from the ranch's accounting books. She had her hair pulled back in one of her braids though a few strands were loose around her neck. Her bare, full lips curled up into an inviting smile, which urged him to taste them. He strode across the floor to her and planted his lips on hers, giving her a thorough kiss.

And was completely unprepared for his heart to roll over in his chest.

"Are you okay?" Shannon said, a worried look in her big brown eyes.

Though he wasn't steady inside at all, he forced a smile and replied lightly, "Of course, *a mhuirnin*." Then, because he needed a few minutes to regain his balance, he straightened with the intention of leaving, but said instead, "Come have dinner with me."

"Are you cooking?" she asked, sounding somewhere between curious and skeptical.

"Hey, I can cook."

She grinned, taunting. "Prove it."

"How do you feel about roast chicken?"

"Generally favorable."

He laughed and rapped his knuckles on the desk lightly. "One hour. Be there." Then he turned and left before he changed his mind and took her on the desk.

It might have been a brief fantasy, but the thought was damn hot.

Knowing there would be time for that later, Sean headed over to his house and got busy prepping for dinner. By the time all the vegetables were cut and added to the chicken and the whole dish was ready for the oven, Sean was revved up and ready to pounce on Shannon the minute she walked in the door. Christ, he wanted that woman. He was beginning to wonder if the feeling would ever lessen in intensity, ever cease.

A little voice inside whispered that it wouldn't, making him sigh in a combination of frustration and resignation. What the feck was he supposed to do with these feelings? There he was, cooking her dinner like they were a normal couple, doing normal couple things. But he knew better than that. It wasn't like he could claim ignorance or stupidity. He knew damn fecking well that he and Shannon had no real future. For crying out loud, she still hadn't come clean about whatever it was that she was hiding. It nagged at him, knowing she was most likely keeping something from him. People didn't usually just show up somewhere with no possessions. Not without reason. He knew that.

But damned if he wasn't going to make her a roast chicken anyway.

Because as much as he knew it was pointless, deep down he *wanted* to be a normal couple with Shannon. If only for a short while. He wanted to pretend that he hadn't spent the last five years of his life living on a foreign continent hiding out under a fake name, always looking over his shoulder. He wanted to forget about all of that and just be fecking normal. When he was with her, it felt possible. Because when he was with her all those fears and worries melted away into nothing, like they'd never existed to begin with.

With Shannon, he could just be.

And for a guy who'd spent the vast majority of his life fighting or hiding, being still and in the moment with a woman was no small thing. But that's what he was discovering with Shannon. *Peace.*

"Knock knock."

Speak of the angel. "Come in, Shannon." His blood stirred knowing she was near. With a deep breath, Sean went to the living room to greet her and to find some music to put on. When he saw her standing in the foyer with her hair down, in a yellow sundress and bare feet, he stopped dead. "You changed," he said, sounding like an idiot.

She smiled at him, blushing. "I found this stuffed in the inside pocket of my duffle bag. I'd forgotten I even had it; it's been missing so long. Anyway, I put it on and thought to myself; well, he *did* ask me to dinner. Why not wear it? So, here I am."

Sean went to her and pulled her into his arms, loving the way her body melted into his. "You look beautiful," he said with complete sincerity. She was the loveliest vision he'd ever seen.

"Thank you, Se—"

Before she could say the rest of his name, he captured her lips in a deep, drugging kiss. And he didn't stop until her arms were around his neck and she was pliant against him. Even then it was hard to stop—*especially* then. The woman he was crazy about was warm and soft and willing.

Forget the fecking chicken. He was hungry for Shannon.

But she had other ideas, unfortunately. With a sexy little moan, she broke the kiss and pulled out of his embrace. Still, the tip of her tongue licked her plump bottom lip like she was searching for one last taste of him and his cock went hard as granite. "I'm starving," she said.

"Me too," he replied, completely serious.

Laughing, she swatted him away playfully when he reached for her. "Food first."

He grinned. "I like the way you think, lass. Boost our energy."

With a *tsk-tsk* over her shoulder, she went to the built-in bookcases that flanked each side of the old brick fireplace and perused the shelves. It hit him then, the way she seemed so comfortable and at home in his living room, and a feeling of rightness washed over him and settled in his heart. He could see it so clearly—in another life this was exactly where they were meant to be.

His gaze roamed over her, and he shook his head, suddenly feeling a little sad.

"You have a lot of old vinyl records, Sean. Are these really yours?" she asked, sounding impressed.

He nodded and gestured to the vintage record player in the corner by the stairs. "They are, yes. After I bought this place I found that player there at a shop in town and brought it back. It reminded me of me mum and growing up in the theaters back in Dublin. She and her cast mates would listen to records for hours while they rehearsed lines and I did my school work."

Shannon glanced over her shoulder at him, her eyes warm and smiling. "That's very sweet."

Shoving his hands in his front pockets to keep them off her because she was obviously not in the mood to be groped by the likes of him—not yet anyway—Sean moved next to her. "Pick one," he said, wondering what she'd choose.

She looked up at him from under her lashes and grinned. "Already did." And she grabbed one off the shelf, holding it to her so he couldn't see. "May I?" she asked, tipping her head toward the player.

"Of course."

As he watched, Shannon pulled the black vinyl record from its cover without letting him see the artist's name, and placed it on the player. With a flick of a switch and an adjustment of the needle, music swelled and filled the room, the sound rich and layered.

Nothing like good ol' vinyl.

Recognizing the song "Tupelo Honey," Sean grinned in approval. "You picked one of my favorites."

Shannon returned his smile and he felt it clear down to his toes. "You're a Van Morrison fan too?"

He nodded. "I am." Then he held a hand out to her, palm up in invitation. "Dance with me?"

She scrunched her nose in the cutest way and said, "Really?" Like she wasn't sure he was serious.

He laughed softly and nodded, so completely drawn to her that he offered up a small secret freely. "Yes, really. I like dancing."

Her eyes went round. "You do?"

She'd been drifting toward him, and she was close enough now for him to grab. Wrapping an arm around her lower back, Sean pulled her close and captured one of her hands in his before they began waltzing slowly to the sultry sound of saxophone. "I'm good at it too."

Shannon tripped at that exact moment but righted herself quickly and laughed, the sound light and carefree as he spun her in lazy circles around the living room. "I can see that."

Then they stopped talking altogether and simply danced in the fading afternoon light, letting their bodies sway in time to the music. Sean pulled her close and held her to him, content and at peace with her in his arms. How was he supposed to ever let her go?

Deeply moved by the realization that he didn't ever want to, he stopped dancing and pulled her in for a kiss that was raw and full of all the emotions he couldn't say.

Overcome by them, he lifted her into his arms and strode to the bedroom, his lips never leaving hers. Though he might not be able to speak his feelings, he could at least show her—*needed* to show her.

And he did, in a coupling that was passionate and emotional and heartfelt. It left both of them wrung out and replete, completely satisfied. Shannon was dozing against him when the oven began to beep, signaling the chicken was finished roasting.

Slipping as quietly as he could from the bed, Sean found his boxers on the floor and dashed to the kitchen, careful to avoid hitting any furniture in the growing dark. Loath to leave Shannon alone for long, he quickly flipped on the light and placed the pan on the stovetop to cool before turning the light off again. He was moving through the living room on his way back to the bedroom and his woman when a muffled sound from behind him made him stop dead in his tracks.

"What the feck?" he muttered under his breath. The hair on the back of his neck rose as his instincts kicked into high alert.

Suddenly there was a loud crash as something fell to the floor. His heart leapt into his throat. Every muscle inside him bunched tight as he spun around. Searching for the cause of the noise, he scanned the room in front of him, eyes searching in the dark for any abnormality. He turned his head to the left just as something big leapt out of the shadows in the far corner toward him moving fast. It hit him and took him down to the floor hard enough to rattle his teeth.

Even as pain exploded behind his eyes, Sean grappled with the intruder. In that moment, every second of the past five years disappeared in a puff of smoke, and he was once again Sean Donaghy, Dublin's bare-knuckle champion. Using every ounce of skill he possessed, he fought hard, throwing punches and using elbows, knees—whatever he had—as adrenaline surged through him. It was almost full dark now and though he couldn't see whom he was attacking, it didn't really matter who it was—only that the person was trying to kill him.

Shannon.

With only the thought of protecting the woman he loved, Sean elbowed his attacker in the solar plexus, pushing his head back, and aiming for his nose. He felt the connection, the give, as bone smashed and blood began gushing everywhere.

His attacker cried out and grabbed for his nose, dropping something that clattered loudly to the ground and skittered across the floor toward his bedroom. Sean could just make out that it was a gun. He started to crawl after it just as his assailant yelled, "Not again, ye fecker!"

Taking the opportunity, Sean rolled onto his feet, his arms up and fists ready, just as Shannon called out from his bedroom, "Sean, are you okay?"

"Stay back!" he yelled in response and swung hard as his attacker came at him again like a charging bull after a red-caped toreador. His fist connected with bone, the impact reverberating all the way up his shoulder. But the intruder didn't go down, only grunted and swore viciously.

Shannon called out, "Lights!" And suddenly the overhead lamp in the living room lit up, temporarily blinding him.

"Feck!" he growled, blinking hard as his pupils struggled to dilate properly. "I can't bloody see!"

"Sean, watch out!" But it was too late. Something hit him from behind, knocking the wind out of him and buckling his knees. As they both began to fall, he finally saw his attacker clearly.

It was his nightmare come to life. "You fecking bastard!"

Billy Hennessey rose to his feet, one shoulder hitched up, blood pumping steadily from his busted nose. "I shoulda killed ye at Belmont when I had the chance," he declared, spitting blood. "Yer a dead man this time, Donaghy."

"It's you!" Shannon yelled unexpectedly, catching everyone's attention. She'd moved and was now on the far side of Sean, with a gun pointed directly across the room at the intruder. "I knew there was something wrong about you. Move and I'll shoot you with your own damn bullets."

Billy sneered at her. "Ye don't have the guts." But he must have decided she might, because he swore in a rapid string of Gaelic and tried to take a step in retreat.

"You know this guy?" Sean asked, confused, but keeping his eyes on Hennessey. How in feck did she know him?

"He spoke to me today at the pet adoption in the park. Said something that made me uncomfortable."

He'd dared to talk to Shannon. Fear slammed into Sean and he yelled at Billy, not even caring what he'd said, "You stay the hell away from her!"

Hennessey shifted onto the balls of his feet, clearly trying to find an escape route.

"I said, don't move!" Shannon yelled, her voice shaking as badly as her hands.

For just a split second Sean took his attention off him and glanced at Shannon, who was once again dressed. But it was long enough. It gave the bastard an opening.

The second Sean's gaze left him, he moved. Hearing him, Sean looked back as Hennessey whipped out the knife he'd concealed behind him and flung it across the room directly at the woman he loved.

"Shannon!" he called out, already in motion.

Her scream split the air as the dagger sliced past her, mere inches from her cheek, and sank deep into the wall behind her. A second later, glass shattered, and Sean caught sight of the hit man escaping through the front window. But he didn't care. He let the bastard go.

Because right then, Shannon hit the floor in a dead faint.

Scrambling to her, Sean dropped to his knees and pulled her into his arms. Panting heavily, he cradled her against him and fought back the terror that was threatening to swallow him whole. "Shannon, wake up. Shannon, please."

But she was still unconscious. Tears stung his eyes as he stared down at her limp in his arms, and the consequences of his choices came back to haunt him. He'd caused this. This was his doing. Shannon's life was in danger because of him. Because he'd been unable to keep her at arm's length. Because he'd been foolish enough to believe that he could have a future.

But there was none waiting for him.

Pulling her even more tightly into his arms as she began to stir, Sean cradled her cheek with a hand and kissed her forehead with trembling lips. There was only one thing he could do now. One thing that would keep her safe and make things right—only it broke his heart.

Shannon had to leave.

Chapter Nineteen

"YOU'RE REALLY FIRING me?"

Shannon still couldn't believe it. Sean was sending her away. Said it was for her own good—her own protection.

It was crushing.

With eyes swimming in tears, she looked at Sean and tried to reach through, to reason with him again. But the way his face was set in such stubborn lines, she had some serious doubts that it would work. But still, she had to try. "I'm truly, sincerely fine, Sean. I didn't hit anything when I fainted and the knife missed me. Other than a slight headache, I'm really okay. You don't need to fire me."

He wasn't swayed. "But I do, and I have. Go back to Saratoga Springs, Shannon, where you belong. Leave me be."

"Why?" Shannon shook her head, completely confused. Maybe it was from fainting, but she didn't think so. "You want me to leave you alone, why? What's going on, Sean? What aren't you telling me? And why did that guy seem to have a history with you? He said 'this time.'"

Her pulse beating thick and heavy, Shannon held her breath and waited for him to answer. But he just stood there with his fists at his sides, that asshole's blood on his boxers, and such a stubborn jaw and hard, determined eyes that she almost gave up then and there and walked away.

But she couldn't. So she waited. And waited.

Until finally he caved. "Feck me—fine. You're as stubborn as me. You want the truth?"

Shannon nodded. "And I want to know why the jerk who attacked you called you Donaghy." There was so much more to this story, she could feel it. "Wait a minute. That guy sounded Irish. You told me once that you got Zeke from a boxing bet in Dublin. Did you *steal* him from that guy?" Is that why the filly was involved? Had Sean done something bad and somebody was getting back at him?

Suddenly, Sean spoke, his voice shaking with emotion. "I didn't bloody feckin' steal anything. I didn't want Zeke! I woke up in that warehouse after losing my fight to find Zeke already there and that bastard about to kill me. I don't know what possessed me, but I looked at Zeke and saw a kindred spirit there. So I took the horse and ran. Can ye fecking blame me for not thinking clearly? I left Ireland that night and I've been hiding in fear for my life ever since and I've fecking *had it*!"

But it was like once he started, he couldn't stop. "So I want you to leave. Because they've found me and they'll hurt you. I can't live with that."

The tears that welled in her eyes fell, one by one, down her cheeks. "So that guy is part of the Irish mob, like a hit man?"

Sean nodded. "Yes."

"And he's been searching for you ever since you left Ireland?"

"Yes."

She wanted to make sure she had it straight. If Sean was making her leave, she wanted to clearly understand why. "Because you got mixed up in a bad bet with the mob boss and took his horse the night he tried to have you killed?"

He cleared his throat. "Basically, yes."

"And now you want me to leave because you think they'll hurt me to get to you?"

"Yes."

"But that guy didn't mention you when he spoke to me earlier. He asked me about my father."

Sean's gaze sharpened. "He did?"

"Yes, and I'm confused. Because if this guy is part of the mob and he only knows you, then how come he was asking me about my dad?"

He shook his dark head wearily. "I don't know."

She thought about it. "There has to be another way."

His face grim, his eyes bleak, Sean replied, "There's not. They know about you now."

"What about going to the police?"

"I'm not exactly legal, Shannon. I've got some forged documents and a fake name—*and* I'm in possession of a horse that had been reported stolen back in Ireland." He pinned her with dark, stormy eyes. "You get the picture

I'm painting? What'll happen if the guards do any digging into me? It was uncomfortable enough having them here when the incident with the filly was reported."

She nodded, her eyes huge. *Holy shit*, was all she could think. "You can't go to the police."

"And you can't stay. We're through, the two of us. We should have never been—never had a chance from the start." He sounded so sad, even though he worked hard to hide it. She could feel his regret like it was a palpable thing.

But she understood why he felt that way, and deep down she agreed. She'd never been honest about anything either. Knowing it was too late, but needing to put it all out there anyway, Shannon took a breath and admitted the truth. "I'm Callum Charlemagne's daughter."

He froze. "You're what?"

"I'm Shannon Charlemagne."

He jerked, clearly disbelieving. "What are you saying?" Now he took a step in retreat, his body rigid.

Scared to death that he was going to hate her, but needing to follow through, she explained. "He sent me here to find out why your horses were racing so well. He's threatened by you. I'm so sorry that I've been lying."

Silence fell and they stared at each other, Shannon trembling slightly as she waited for his response. It seemed like forever before he even moved.

"It can't matter now. Please leave," he finally said quietly, his face impassive, his eyes dark with unspoken emotion. "You have to, Shannon."

She didn't want to—God, no. She didn't want to at *all*—but she did.

She left Sean standing in his living room, with a broken front window and her heart shattered into a million pieces like the glass at his feet.

"HE FIRED ME, Dad. I'm sorry," Shannon stated and sat on the bed at Fortune's local B&B the next day. After she'd gotten a ride into town from Tim, she'd gone directly to the old Victorian at the end of Main Street. She could have gone anywhere—the donut shop, the coffee place down the street, or even the brewpub—but instead, she'd chosen to just get a room because deep down she simply wasn't ready to leave…even if Sean wanted her to. "I got a room at the Sweetbriar Inn, so I'm still here in town."

Callum Charlemagne exploded, his voice blaring through the phone. "Fired? You got *fired*? How in the hell did you let that happen, Shannon? I was counting on you!"

Anxiety flooded her, froze her momentarily in place. It scrambled her system and had her stammering to apologize before she even knew what she was doing. But as soon as she opened her mouth to say she was sorry, an image of Sean crossed her brain and something inside made her stop.

Shannon opened her mouth again and instead of an apology, she blurted out quickly before she lost courage, "You never should have made me do this in the first place, Dad. This isn't my fault."

"Excuse me?" her father said with an exaggerated drawl. "How is this not your fault? You were fired, Shannon. Not me."

She closed her eyes and said the one truth she should have from the beginning. "You should have never sent me." She saw that now very clearly.

Her father scoffed. "Clearly."

Shannon frowned, not liking the tone of his voice. "What does that mean?"

Callum sighed in the receiver, his voice deep and filled with restrained anger. "It means I'm flying to Fortune. Stay put. I'll call you when I get there."

The line went dead.

Shannon was left with nothing to do but wait.

"THANKS FOR COMING," Sean said as he opened to the door and waved Jake and Aidan inside. It had been less than a day since he'd made Shannon leave and he was downright miserable. Knowing that sending her away had been the right thing to do didn't make his feelings any easier to bear. Christ, what he wouldn't give to have her in his arms again.

That's why he'd called the guys.

After cleaning up the mess from the broken window, he'd spent the rest of the night tossing and turning even though he hadn't been able to stop from texting her to make sure she was safe before he'd gone to bed. Even when she'd texted back that she was, it hadn't helped him sleep. In the dark hours before dawn he'd made a decision: It was time to take a stand. The only way he'd ever have a full life was if he stopped hiding from his past and faced it head on.

It was the only way he could have Shannon.

And even though she'd dropped that bombshell on him about being that bastard Charlemagne's daughter, his heart was hers. Completely and totally. Forever. Granted, there were many things to sort out, but he just couldn't take Shannon for the manipulative, lying type. Not of her own free will anyway. Because all the ways in which she got so nervous and fidgeted so often, or sported red-rimmed eyes from crying in secret, hadn't escaped him.

Yes, he'd noticed, all right. And his heart went out to her because he'd seen that behavior before in others—he'd seen it in his mom. He knew that it meant Shannon dealt with a lot of worries in that beautiful head of hers. And he could only imagine what having Callum Charlemagne for a parent had done to her.

And now, all he wanted to do was hold her until she was better.

But he couldn't do that until he was free.

Kicking the door shut, Sean raked a hand through his dark hair and opened his mouth to speak, but Jake cut him off. "You look like shit, man."

Yeah, well, he kind of felt like it, too.

"Oh, and I brought this," his mate added, and lifted up an enormous glass jug full of liquid. "I was helping Grandpop fix his distillery when I got your call. He overheard us talking and decided I should bring you some of his homemade moonshine to help ease your tension." Jake smirked, holding the jug out to him. "Backyard contraband, compliment of Harvey Stone."

Sean took the big jug, surprised at just how heavy it was. "Thanks, mate. I might need this."

"Careful with it, though." Aidan chimed in then as he sat down on the overstuffed couch. "That stuff will have you dumb as a post and howling at the moon after just a few shots. His granddad doesn't joke round with his homemade liquor."

Jake grinned wide. "Remember that time in high school when we swiped his hooch because you were too nervous to ask Becky Hartwell to the prom and wanted some liquid courage?"

Aidan nodded his auburn head, looking mildly pained. "How could I forget? I was so keyed up over that girl and wanted to make a good impression. But after three shots of that stuff I was so wrecked that I knocked on the door and ended up asking out her mother instead of her."

"Funniest thing of all was that she said yes," Jake replied, laughing at the memory.

"Please don't remind me," Aidan groaned. "I'm just glad that Mr. Hartwell let me leave in one piece after showing up drunk and hitting on his wife." He glanced at them both. "That man still scowls when he sees me on the streets."

Sean broke into their banter, the heaviness of his situation weighing him down. It was time to do something about it. And there was just no easy way to come out and say it, so, "I'm in trouble and I need your help."

That got their attention.

He looked at Jake. "Not too long ago you asked me when I was ever going to tell you the truth. Well, now's the time."

For all of Jake's grumbling, he was a damn good friend, so Sean wasn't surprised when he placed a reassuring hand on his shoulder. "Whatever you need. We're here to help."

Aidan instantly nodded in agreement. "What can we do?"

Because he didn't know how else to say it, Sean began to pace the living room and just started rambling. "You both know I was boxer back in Dublin, right?"

They nodded and Jake crossed his arms over his chest. "Yeah. Continue."

Whew. This was hard. "I got mixed up in an illegal betting ring run by the mob just before my last fight—the one that I lost. The mob boss had a lot of money riding on it and thought that by making a side bet with me, I wouldn't lose, that he could put some added pressure on me. You know, make me perform better, scare me into winning?" He shook his head, remembering. "Anyway, it didn't work. I lost the boxing match and at the same time won the bet with O'Banion."

Aidan interjected, "What was the bet?"

"Zeke," Sean replied. "He bet me Zeke."

"So that's why you showed up in town with no other possessions besides that colt."

Sean nodded. "Yes. I got knocked out that night, and when I regained consciousness I discovered I was in an old abandoned warehouse with O'Banion's favorite hit man. He was about to kill me with Zeke standing in the corner."

Jake frowned. "I don't get it. Why was the horse there?"

"It was for show, really. O'Banion never meant to give me his horse. At any rate, his guy—Billy Hennessey—pulled out a knife and I attacked him. I knocked him out and, without thinking, grabbed Zeke and ran."

"O'Banion must not have been very happy about that," he commented.

Sean stopped pacing and pegged him with a look. "That's why I'm in trouble. He found me."

"Fuck."

He nodded and resumed pacing. "Notice the cardboard over the window there?" He hooked his thumb at the busted window. "Billy shattered it when he attacked me and Shannon last night."

Both men shot to their feet. "Where's Shannon?"

"Safe." Thank God. "I sent her back to New York."

"What happened to the guy who attacked you? Did he get away?" Aidan asked as he moved to inspect the broken window.

"Billy did, yes. The bastard's the same guy I fought that night back in Dublin."

"Wait. Is that the guy whose face you messed up? The reflection you thought you saw at the pub?" Jake asked.

"Yes."

"Shit."

Pretty much. "I'm done, Jake. I'm really done running and hiding from these feckers. And that's why I need your help."

Jake rubbed his hands together and smiled, his dark eyes full of bad intentions. "Oh, we'll help all right. We'll get you untangled from this mess. But first off, we should call the police."

Sean grimaced. "Can't do that, mate. I'm here on forged documents under a false name. I'm not really legal, you see." He gave him a pained look. "My real name is Sean Donaghy. So no police, please."

Aidan looked over his shoulder at them. "You can count on us, brother."

Relief hit Sean then and nearly buckled his knees. He hadn't realized how much hearing that was going to mean to him. "Thank you."

"Hey, we took you in when you first arrived and made you a part of our family. No way we'd turn our back on you now," Jake said seriously. "You're one of us."

Moved, Sean pulled the pub owner to him for a brief, hard hug. "Thanks, mate."

"No thanks needed," his friend replied, clapping him on the back before releasing him. "Now all we need is a plan."

"Right." He hadn't actually gotten that far.

Just then a sound came from outside and all three men swiveled their heads in the direction it came from, their bodies growing still.

"What the hell was that?" Aidan said.

At that moment the front door flew opened and slammed against the wall. Three masked men rushed into the room, holding guns. Before Sean had time to react one of them grabbed him by the arm and pointed a gun at his temple. Panic leapt into his throat.

"Yer coming with me," the masked man said in an Irish accent. Then to the other men he said, "Grab these other two. We'll take them too."

Both Aidan and Jake already had their hands in the air and were standing very still.

Hoping to distract them from his friends, Sean found his voice and demanded, "What do you want?"

"Why, yer prize horse, of course!" the thug currently pointing a gun at his head replied. "We've come to kidnap him just like we did his grandsire. Haven't you read your history?"

Zeke? The men were after Zeke? Is that what they'd been intending all along when they'd injured him at Belmont—to ruin his racing career, then steal him like they had Shergar and make him stand stud on O'Banion's farm?

No fecking way.

Moving unexpectedly against the intruder, Sean grabbed the man's wrist and squeezed down as hard as he could. His attacker cried out in pain and dropped the gun. Sean rounded on him and slammed his fist into his face, rammed his knee into his groin, and was already turning to help his friends when he crumpled to the ground.

But they were already in motion.

Jake had snatched the heavy jug off the coffee table and slammed his guy upside the temple with it, dropping him like a rock and taking his gun. Then he turned to assist Aidan, who was dashing out the front door after the third masked man he'd just succeeded in disarming, the gun still skidding across the floor. Cursing, Jake sprinted after him, jug still in hand. Sean snatched the gun up from the floor, and wasn't far behind.

They'd just leapt from the porch when Aidan caught up to the intruder by the bed of his truck. Piles of wood hung out the back and Aidan reached for one, grabbing a scrap two-by-four and swung it like a baseball bat. He nailed the masked man on the back of the head and sent him sprawling face-first into the gravel. "Get up, you bastard!" he hollered, standing over the prone figure, his chest heaving.

At that moment a loud crash came from inside the barn where Zeke was housed and horses began to stomp and whinny and neigh. Sean left the guys with the downed thugs and was in motion, flying through the small stand of aspens and over the expanse of grass that separated the house from the barns in an instant. As he closed in on the building, the barn door swung wide and three more masked men came hurtling out, Zeke right behind them. The horse was rearing and stomping and making all kinds of ruckus. One of the thieves tripped and fell.

"Help me!" he yelled to his partners and raised his hands up over his face in a protective motion as he tried to scoot away. Zeke reared up over him, his hooves glinting in the sunlight, his eyes huge and white-rimmed.

But the other men were already halfway across the grass.

"Please, don't leave me!" He cried out as Zeke's hooves came crashing down, missing him by just inches. The horse's halter rope slapped him in the face.

Rushing forward, Sean shoved the gun in his waistband and gathered the loose rope, pulling his horse back from the fallen man. "Here," he said to Jake who'd just arrived. "Hold him." He handed the lead to his mate and spun on the intruder.

Yanking him up by the collar, Sean stared into blank eyes and shook him hard. "Where's Hennessey?" he demanded. The thug just smiled. So Sean punched him hard in the gut. "Tell me where Hennessey is!" he yelled again. Billy had to be around somewhere.

The thug doubled over coughing and sputtered between gasps, "He knows your broad's in town and he's looking for her."

Shannon.

Cold dread swamped him. "How does he know where she is?"

"Does it matter?"

Not in that instant, so he let the masked man go. He didn't stop him when he leapt up and began racing away. It was probably a mistake, but the only thing his mind registered was that Shannon was in danger. He had to find her.

Tim came bursting through the gap between barns then, panting hard. "What's going on? Is everybody safe?"

Not yet.

Sean pointed at Zeke, who was still wide-eyed and snorting but was standing calm with Jake. "Take him and don't let him out of your sight."

Just then Aidan arrived and said as he tucked the third gun in the waistband of his jeans, "Found this in the house. Also, I took care of the masked jackasses and tied them to that huge oak tree in your front yard with some bungee cord I had in my truck."

Sean shot him a look of thanks and said as he turned back to Tim, "Call the police. They can handle the thugs." Then he turned to his brothers. "You two come with me. We've got to find Shannon."

He didn't wait to see if they'd follow because he knew they would.

Family protected what they loved.

And he, he loved Shannon. His beautiful, sweet Shannon. Whom he'd sent away in an attempt to keep safe but was now in even more danger. She was alone and vulnerable with a killer after her.

So he ran.

Chapter Twenty

THE SUN WAS just starting to set behind Jasper's Peak when Shannon's father texted that he was in town: "Meet me in an hour. Your room."

Why was she doing this? Why was she letting herself be bossed around and told what to do like she was a little girl? None of his reasoning for sending her after Sean made any sense. In fact, none of any of this made any freaking sense at all!

"So why the hell am I doing it?" Shannon said aloud as she hit the pavement in front of the Sweetbriar and started walking down the sidewalk. Her insides were twisted into knots over the whole thing, and she was so wound up that she couldn't sit still. And now that she had an hour to kill, she decided to take a walk. Better than sitting around, spinning out and crying about everything. There was too much to process anyway, and it wasn't going to happen in the time it took to fold a load of laundry. After she dealt with her father and whatever he wanted, then she could fall apart and weep for a week.

Noticing June from the co-op up ahead with a group of ladies, Shannon ducked into a small alley between two buildings. There was no way she could be social right now—not with her emotions all over the place. Maybe later, but for now she was apparently going to explore Fortune's treasures off Main Street.

Forcing her attention onto her surroundings and out of the static in her head, Shannon entered a charming older neighborhood filled with enormous trees and turn-of-the-century bungalows. Lilacs in varying shades of purple bloomed alongside roses, creating a colorful display. As she walked down the quiet street, she noticed that a few alleys split off from the main road. She was just looking down one that opened up between two huge bushes to her right when movement caught her eye. A person in a dark hooded sweatshirt opened up a wooden gate and slipped into a private, fenced back yard.

Blinking hard, Shannon shook her head in denial, but her stomach plummeted. She knew what—*who*—she'd just seen. And there had been blood on his jeans.

Sean's attacker, Billy Hennessey.

Without thinking, Shannon turned down the side alley and slowed her pace to a leisurely stroll. She wanted to see if she could catch anything between the fence's boards when she passed. As she drew closer, she could make out the sound of people talking.

Reaching the property line, Shannon noticed the large garbage and recycling cans that were set near the gate. She crouched down near them, hiding herself, and pretended like her shoelace was untied. As she retied it, she looked through the space between the boards directly in front of her.

At first she couldn't make out much of anything as her eyes struggled to adjust to the narrowed perspective. Then she could see a simple grass lawn and concrete patio. There were no personal effects around the yard, no toys or tools or ornaments. The only items in the small space were a glass-top patio table and chairs. Mostly the place looked empty.

Was Sean's attacker breaking and entering?

But just then a loud creak sounded as the back screen door swung open. The sleaze Hennessey who'd hurt Sean stepped out onto the concrete patio. Just seeing him made her stomach squeeze painfully and had fear skittering up her spine.

He had dead eyes.

He was speaking quickly, but his accent was thick and she had a hard time making out what he was saying. Momentarily frustrated, she was about to stand up and look for a closer spot where she could hear better, when it occurred to her that she had her cell phone on her. And it had recording capabilities.

"Duh, Shannon." She muttered under her breath and pulled it from the back pocket of her jeans.

A dog barked to her left suddenly and she jumped, her already rapid pulse going haywire. Almost panting, Shannon fumbled with her phone until she found the camera app and tapped it open, then hit the little video camera in the bottom corner. Then she held it up and focused it on the hit man through the gap in the boards. She just hoped that the mic might pick up what she wasn't able to hear on her own.

With her gaze swapping back and forth between her phone display and watching the real thing, she didn't notice the door creak open again. Didn't notice the two men who stepped out of the house until they came into focus on her phone. But when they did she let out a small cry of anguish. It couldn't be!

Shannon looked from her display through the board gap and back, not wanting to believe it. But no matter how much she wanted it to be different, the proof was right there being recorded on her phone. Only she didn't know what it meant—except that it had to be really, really bad.

Because there on her display—and there in person—was her father, Callum Charlemagne, standing next to a short, stocky, barrel-chested man and Billy Hennessey. They were deep in conversation and she strained to hear what they were saying.

"Do ye have what ye owe me?" the other guy said, speaking in his heavy Irish accent.

"I don't have your money, O'Banion. Not yet anyway."

O'Banion? Wait a minute.

The man lit a cigarette and took a drag. "Well, now, that's bloody unfortunate."

Her father held out his hands in supplication and said in a voice she'd never heard before—a scared one. "Mickey, please. I've done everything you've asked of me over the years, ever since I first got into debt with you. I've made good, haven't I?"

O'Banion laughed, the sound as warm as a block of ice. "Not even feckin' close. Do you really think that using your farm's stud fees to launder me money is enough to make good on all the money you've borrowed over the years? Christ, ye been gambling me own fecking money! Ye think that don't make me pissed?" The mob boss spat on the ground, his face contorting angrily. "If I didn't need yer fecking farm for me business, I'd have slaughtered ye like a pig already."

Her father went pale at that and he pointed at his chest emphatically, though his hand was trembling. "*I am the one who discovered Sean Muldoon for you after making the connection between his horse and Shergar. You should be thanking me.*" He ended, his voice weak and shaky.

Shannon went very still as something occurred to her, something that made her stomach uneasy. Is that why her father had gotten weird when she'd mentioned Sean's boxing days? He'd told her the information was helpful. And now that she thought back on it, he'd sounded almost excited too. And then he'd hung up on her. God, had that seemingly innocent information actually been an important clue in locating Sean?

How would she ever make it up to him if she were the reason he'd been discovered?

"Aye, it's true ye did," O'Banion said, taking another drag off his cigarette. "And I do love me racehorses. Ye did good, and me men should be retrieving me long lost baby from that snake Donaghy now." He glared at Hennessey. "If ye hadn't bungled yer kidnapping at Belmont, he'd be back at me stud farm already. But ye did kill his new foal to make it up to me, right? The filly? Ye said ye did and ye'd better not have lied to me. Ye know what I do with liars."

"Aye, I handled it." Hennessey muttered, looking away uneasily, and changed the subject. "At least I got a shot in on Donaghy while I was at the race. But that fecker and I aren't finished for what he did to me face."

He grunted. "Bastard made ye prettier if he ask me." Then he grinned at his own joke and turned back to her father, his face showing his disdain. "The two of us, we ain't square yet. Not even close."

Her father looked around, his eyes huge and darting about wildly. "I'll do whatever it takes."

"Ye really mean that?"

Her father nodded, his face going from pale to ashen. "Yes. Anything to make us even."

O'Banion eyed her father, his expression one of interest. "I did miss me horse. What else ye got?" Then his face changed and his eyes went deadly serious. "Impress me."

"I'll kill Sean Muldoon."

Her butt dropped to the ground as her knees gave out and her world crashed around her. The words made her blood run cold—made her want to scream. Her father had looked at the mobster and said them simply, easily. He'd spoken words that would be branded into her brain for all eternity. Four little words that shattered her reality.

IN TOWN, SEAN, Jake, and Aidan canvassed the area looking for Shannon. With any luck she'd already caught a flight out of Fortune and was home safe. But Sean wasn't taking any chances. Not after Tim told him he'd dropped her at the Sweetbriar and that thug had said Hennessey knew she was still in town. The B&B had been the first place they'd searched, only to come up empty.

For what seemed like hours they ran down this street and that one, searching for any glimpse of Shannon or Hennessey. Running on adrenaline alone, Sean slipped down a side alley and came to an abrupt stop. "Oh, thank God," he declared. He'd told her to go, but she hadn't listened. He was too happy to see her safe to care.

There was Shannon plain as day, crouched by a pair of garbage cans, her face devoid of color and her eyes blank with shock. In an instant he was kneeling beside her, his hands cupping her cheeks that had gone cold as ice.

"Shannon," he whispered raggedly. "Talk to me."

She seemed to look right through him, but said in a small voice, "I'm so sorry."

Confused and worried, Sean forgot about tracking Billy and tried to pull Shannon into his arms, because really, she was the only thing that mattered. Her entire body was shaking. But she jerked when he touched her, so he stopped. "What are you sorry for, *a mhuirnin*?"

"I lied to you," she said softly, her eyes huge and dark with emotion. "But I didn't know. I swear I didn't know."

Searching her face earnestly, Sean asked, "What are you talking about, Shannon? I don't understand."

Instead of explaining she pointed to the gap in the fence. "Look."

Shifting on his heels as Aidan and Jake arrived, the two men breathing heavily from exertion, he leaned around her and cursed swiftly at what he saw. It was his worst nightmare come to life. Right there in front of him in real time. "Shite! O'Banion and Hennessey. With Callum Charlemagne, that bastard. I knew he wasn't right. What the feck is he doing with those two?"

"He's my father," Shannon said, her voice flat and void of emotion.

"I know, love. I'm sorry."

Her lips pressed together and her chin began to quiver. "I didn't know what he was involved in, Sean, I swear. I wouldn't have agreed if I had known."

Anger, betrayal, fear. Emotions reared up inside him over Shannon's manipulation, and he knew he'd have to acknowledge and sort through them at some point, but right then he only wanted to know one thing. "Did you set me up, Shannon?" He wasn't sure he could handle it if she had. Not the woman he loved.

Her eyes never left his as she shook her head vehemently. "No! I had no idea what my father was involved in."

Taking a deep breath, he replied, "Okay, then explain to me what you were doing." He wanted to believe in her innocence. Wanted to believe in her goodness.

She swiped at the tears on her cheeks with the back of a hand and said, "Our company is on the brink of bankruptcy, and he led me to believe it's your fault. That we've lost almost all our clients to your breeding program over the past few years and had to borrow against our stock to keep the operation going. But now we can't repay the loan. He told me he was convinced you're doping your horses and he wanted me to find proof. And I believed him because he's my father."

A dark, bitter smile curled his lips. "Did you find what you came looking for?"

She shook her head, concern furrowing her brow. "I didn't, no. But Sean, I didn't even look very hard."

"Well now, that's a relief." His voice dripped sarcasm.

"I meant that I knew you were innocent. Please believe me."

How was he supposed to believe anything? Her father was in bed with the Irish mob. The very men who wanted him dead. "I don't know what to believe." That much was the truth.

Shannon reached out and placed a trembling hand on his knee. "Then just listen while I finish explaining before making any decisions, please. That was the story my father told me, but that's not the truth." She paused and took a deep, slow breath before continuing. "He lied. I just saw and heard the real story. The truth is he's a gambling addict. He got in deep with O'Banion and used our farm as a front to launder mob money in an attempt to make things right. But my father kept gambling away all our money *and* the mob's, and now he's in really big trouble with them. I see now that the real reason he sent me out here wasn't because he'd wanted me to find dirt on you. It was to locate Zeke because he knew the truth about him and he was going to give both of you up to O'Banion in exchange for his debt being wiped clean." She fisted her hands in her lap. "It makes me angry that I was used and manipulated like that, but it's the honest truth."

His heart squeezed tight at the sight of her beautiful eyes looking so bleak. "I don't know, Shannon." Even if he did believe her, how did it change anything?

"I've spent years worrying and trying to please him. I wanted so much for him love me again like he had when I was little that I put up with his bullying. I never stood up for myself. And all that time he's been nothing but a liar and a thief." Suddenly, Shannon shot to her feet, her face set in determined lines. "I'll prove it."

He hissed, "Get back here, damn it."

"Don't be foolish," Aidan demanded. "Stay put and let us handle this."

She just shook her head at them as she seemed to resolve something inside. Her shoulders went back and her spine straightened. "No," she said emphatically to him. "I'm right about you. And I'm not backing down from him this time. I'm done living in fear of his rejection and disapproval, and allowing that to dictate my life. Because I've learned that my perspective is valuable and valid, whether he approves of it or not. And I don't need him to—not anymore. I'm going to prove I know you're innocent. In fact, I'm going to put an end to this whole fucking thing right now."

Fear seized him when she turned and placed her hand on the back gate latch. "Shannon, don't be stupid."

Something flashed in her eyes, and she seemed to grow stronger, more determined right in front of him.

"That's just it, Sean. I've been stupid for far too long. Now I'm going to make things right. Stay right here."

Before he could stop her, she swung the gate wide open and said loudly, "Hiya, Dad! Imagine seeing you here!"

"Feck!" He was on his feet, his heart lodged firmly in his throat. That was the woman he loved, regardless of how she'd come to him.

And she'd just walked into a death trap.

SHANNON HAD NEVER felt more determined or more angry than she did at that moment. Her hands shook violently, but she strolled across the cool green grass to the three men on the patio who were currently staring at her like she was an alien.

"So, Daddy. Care to tell me what you're doing here with these men?"

Her father looked completely flummoxed, his face going five shades of red before he stammered, "Why, Sh-Sh-Shannon, what a surprise! What are you doing here?"

Pasting a fake smile on her face even as her insides seethed, she forced a casual tone. "Well, see, I was just taking a walk since you didn't want to meet for another half hour or so." She gave him a wide-eyed innocent look. "Now I see why. You had another meeting."

The stocky man called O'Banion tipped his chin and said gruffly, "Ye'd best get out of here, lass. This isn't where you belong."

Shannon had to disagree. "Actually, it is. Sorry." Part of her was amazed at her courage and could hardly believe what she was doing. But she'd heard of the amazing feats people could accomplish when properly motivated.

Saving Sean's life was a damn good motivation.

Her father must have regained some composure, because he said in that cold, condescending tone of his that never failed to set her off, "Do as you're told, girl."

Then something inside her snapped. "No!"

His bushy eyebrows shot into his hairline. "Excuse me?"

But she didn't hear anything else because a whole life-time of putting up with his bullying and abuse while she'd kept her mouth shut was coming out. "I said no! I'm not listening to you anymore. My whole life I've done every-thing you asked, no questions. And what has it gotten me? A lifetime of insecurity and a fucking anxiety disorder!"

"Now that's not my fault."

Her mouth dropped open and she sputtered, fuming at his automatic rejection of accountability. But it'd been that way her whole life and she was done. Just fucking *done*.

"Oh really? It's not your fault? Why, because you've never shouted, belittled, or abused me and Colleen? Because you're such a stellar specimen of humanity?" She scoffed, continuing, "That's bullshit. You haven't been a father to me since I was a girl. Ever since you took that business trip to Ireland and came back a different man. But you know what? That's fine. You can believe what you want because I'm done with you."

Her father scowled hotly, clearly not happy about being dressed down in front of these men by his daugh-ter. "I'm your father, young lady. How dare you talk to me this way?"

"How dare I?" Shannon sputtered. "How dare *I?*" Marching up to her father she poked him right in the center of his chest. Hard. "How dare *you!*"

Reaching into her pocket she yanked out her phone and hit the play button on the video she'd recorded. In stunned silence her father, the mob boss, and the hit man watched themselves on video as they planned their hit on Sean.

"Seen enough?" she demanded after a few moments. "I know I have. Oh, and in case you're wondering, I've already emailed this clip and have copies." She'd made sure to have backups. Though she was acting more rash than she ever had in her life, she wasn't that stupid—even if her outward demeanor might suggest otherwise. Minutes before Sean had arrived, she'd managed to email the clip to herself and to Colleen with strict instructions to wait for a signal from Shannon. One simple, blank text from her and her sister would be on the phone with the police immediately. Though she really hoped it wouldn't come to that, because it would bring Sean under scrutiny and she didn't want an investigation started on him.

Suddenly all three men looked past her shoulder and she heard someone approaching. "Shannon, stop," Sean said from a few feet behind her, Aidan and Jake at his side. "What do you think you're doing?"

She glanced over her shoulder and her heart filled with emotion for him. "I'm saving our life," she said simply.

"Our life?" He shook his head warily, his gaze moving from her to the other men and back. "I don't understand."

And she could see that he didn't. Well, that she could explain. "It's simple, Sean. I love you."

"The hell you do," Callum said.

She turned to her father. "You don't get to decide my feelings. Or my life anymore, for that matter. I love Sean." She glanced over her shoulder to where he was standing, green eyes wide and his mouth a little gaped. She winked. "Get used to it," she said lightly, a little amazed at her own boldness. "I'm going to be saying it a lot."

Sean just looked at her, stammering, "Umm, okay?"

"When we're all done, here you can reciprocate and tell me that you love me too. I'll let you."

That got a grin out of him. And a short laugh. And a shake of his head like he didn't know what to make of her. "You got a deal." Then he glanced over her head toward the men on the patio. "How about we extricate ourselves from this little situation first though, love?"

Why she felt so confident suddenly, she wasn't sure, but deep down in her heart she knew her father wouldn't let anyone harm them. If only because she had that video. "Here's what's going to happen," she started and turned back to Mickey O'Banion and Billy Hennessey. "You're going to forget about Sean. You're going to turn right around and leave, going back to whatever rock you live under in Ireland. This vendetta you have against him is done. Finished."

Billy sneered at Sean, his face bruised and his already mashed nose swollen something terrible. She didn't feel sorry for him. "It ain't over."

She just raised a brow, giving her best regal expression. "Oh, I think it is. Because if it isn't, I'm going to broadcast this video all over the fucking Internet, after I take it to the cops, my dear. We can let the police and the whole world see you planning a hit on the man I love."

He glared at her hard through puffy, blackened eyes, but fell silent. Next she turned to O'Banion and her father. "And I think there are a lot of people who'd be real interested in learning how you two are in business together." To her father she added, "I'm seriously disappointed in you. You raised me to be a good, honest person full of integrity. You're nothing but a liar and a fake."

"Shannon," her father said, his tone conciliatory. But she knew better by now than to buy it.

Walking backward across the grass, she shook her head at her father, stopping when she reached Sean's side. "No," she said again. *Just, no.*

A large, hard hand grabbed hers and held it tight. Glancing up, she smiled at the expression in Sean's eyes. Looked like he believed her after all. "I told you, Sean."

The man of her dreams squeezed her hand and whispered back, "I believe you." And then he glanced at the men, clearly uneasy. "How about we get the feck away from here?"

Shannon couldn't agree more. But first, "Do we have a deal?" she said to her father and his accomplices. "Sean's freedom for our silence."

At that moment, Hennessey moved quickly, a single blur of motion, and threw a knife directly at Shannon.

"No!" Sean said, leaping in front of her. Aidan and Jake yelled and rushed toward her too.

The knife sunk into Sean's left shoulder and Shannon screamed. When she glimpsed a shiny piece of metal in his waistband as he began to slump to the ground, she grabbed the gun he'd shoved there, raised it, and in blind panic, fired a single shot.

"What the feck?" Hennessey said as bright red bloomed on the front of his shirt. He looked at her father, his face filled with disbelief. "I think she got me." Then he crumpled to the ground as he passed out from the bullet going clean through his side.

Her father looked from her to O'Banion, and back. "Shannon, what did you do? You just shot him!"

She didn't pay him any attention. She was already crouching next to Sean, Aidan and Jake standing guard over them with guns in their hands, raised and aimed steady on O'Banion. "Stay with me," she ordered feeling more thankful than she could ever say to have the guys' strong display of protection and support.

"We're going to get you out of here, Sean," Aidan stated matter-of-factly, his eyes dark and stormy. "Just hold on."

Though his expression was pained, Sean replied with a strong, true voice. "I'm not going anywhere. It'll take more than a flesh wound to get me." He pulled the knife from his shoulder and let it drop to the ground with a clang.

Thank God.

"That's my boy," Jake said.

Noticing she was still holding the gun, Shannon rose to her feet and immediately felt Aidan and Jake move to her side, the three of them a united wall around Sean. Raising her hand, she aimed the gun right at O'Banion's chest. "You want to be next?" she demanded, not entirely sure if she was kidding. "Or do we have a deal?"

O'Banion lifted his hands, palm out in a display of surrender, and nodded curtly. Funny how having three guns leveled on him and his trusty hit man bleeding and unconscious at his feet suddenly made him real open to negotiation. "We have a deal."

Relief flooded her. "Great." Feeling triumphant, she added a warning to her father: "You'll be hearing from me."

"I'm so sorry, Shannon. I never meant—"

But she cut him off because she didn't want to hear it. "Save it. You're not my father." As Hennessey started to moan, she said to O'Banion, "Your guy needs help."

"Let's get out of here," Sean whispered raggedly from the ground.

Shannon nodded. "Let's do."

Jake and Aidan helped Sean to his feet while keeping their guns leveled on O'Banion.

As soon as he was standing, Jake said, "I've had lots of practice stitching up my old man. I can fix that wound right up. Let's get you back to my place."

Together they slipped from the backyard, walking fast. They kept up the pace until they'd reached Main Street. When they were standing in front of Two Moons, Sean stopped suddenly.

"What is it?" she asked, her heart pounding fast and unsteady. Had she really just done all of that? Had she really just stood up to her father, a mobster—and gained Sean's freedom?

Yes, yes she had.

It was unsettling. Scary. *Liberating.*

And, although it was going to take some time to sort through all of the feelings running through her at the moment, she knew deep down that she'd done the right thing. Standing there in the sunshine with Sean, alive and together, was proof of that.

He pulled her close. She loved the feel of his arms around her. In fact, she could get used to it for, oh, she didn't know—the rest of her life. God, she loved this man. Truly. Deeply.

"Shannon?"

She snuggled closer. "Yes?"

"Thank you."

"I love you." It was that simple.

"Me too," he said soft and sweet against her ear.

Butterflies launched in her tummy, but she couldn't help teasing because she wanted to hear the words. "That's not proper reciprocity, Sean."

He pulled back and took her head in his hands, his expression suddenly very serious. "I love you, Shannon. You are my first and only. For the rest of my life, if you want me."

She'd take that.

Yeah, she'd definitely take that. Rising on her toes, she kissed him tenderly and then pulled back to look him in the eyes because what she was about to say was huge. It was life-altering.

"Sean?"

"Yes, love?"

She broke out in a huge smile. She couldn't help it. It just felt so darn good to say it.

"I choose you."

Epilogue

Two Moons was bursting at the seams. It was Saturday night, and karaoke was in full swing as Shannon made her way to the bar where she'd spotted Sean. It had been three months since the showdown with the Bad Men, as she now referred to them. Three glorious months of a life that was all hers. Well, and Sean's. Since that day they'd been inseparable.

Love was awesome.

"Hey," she said in greeting and plopped onto a stool next to him, giving him a kiss on the cheek. "Sorry I'm late. Did I miss anything?"

Jake was pulling a pint from tap and said gruffly, "Apple. You missed Apple."

"Really? Did she sing again?" She spun on her stool looking between both men. "Was she drunk?"

Sean nodded and laughed. Jake nodded and scowled.

She was hit with a pang of disappointment. "Was it as good as last time?"

Her man laughed. "Yep."

Jake swore and tossed his towel on the bar. "Cold-hearted snake, my ass."

Shannon burst into laughter. "Is that was she sang?"

Her cell phone rang, and she reached into her purse, pulling it out. Seeing that it was Colleen, she covered one ear with her hand and answered. "Hey, Leenie."

"Shannon?" her sister said in a voice that was shaking terribly and unusually high-pitched. "Shannon, what am I going to do?"

Worry gripped her. Colleen never sounded like this. She never sounded scared. "What's going on? What happened?"

"Y-you don't know?"

"What don't I know?" Shannon felt anxiety start to rear its head. Shit. She hadn't had a single episode in three months. "What's going on, Colleen?"

Her sister hiccupped into the phone and sniffled loudly. "Turn on the TV. It's all over the news."

What was all over the news? "Hold on," she said into the phone before turning to Jake. "Can you turn on the TV please?"

Jake gave her a questioning look, but complied, and when Shannon got a good look at the breaking news report plastered across the screen, she nearly dropped the phone. "Holy shit," she whispered.

There on the television were her father and Mickey O'Banion. It was showing them on screen, each being hauled from the stables at the Saratoga Springs racetrack in handcuffs. The headline flashing across the screen read, AMERICAN HORSERACING LEGEND CALLUM CHARLEMAGNE ARRESTED IN SUSPECTED CONNECTION TO MOB LAUNDERING SCHEME.

"Do you see?" Colleen demanded.

Though it was hard to speak, Shannon managed, "I do. But I don't understand what's happening."

"The police found some incriminating evidence against Dad, Shannon. It's bad. First they discovered a trail of money transfers and deposits from overseas bank accounts that linked him to O'Banion. Then they obtained a warrant for the house and found hidden in a safe all of Dad's falsified books that expose the whole dirty scheme they were in on together. The company has been seized and all of the family assets frozen. It's a nightmare. He's looking at jail, Shan. I want to feel bad about it, but it's hard, knowing everything he did, all the ways he lied and cheated us for years. The way he used you. It makes it hard to be too sympathetic, you know? And Mom's freaking out and has already packed her bags. She says she's going to Cancún and isn't coming back until this is all over. And I'm so screwed. I just got a call from administration at Harvard and there's no money to pay for med school. They've suspended me. What am I going to do?"

Closing her eyes, Shannon inhaled long and deep and reached for Sean's hand, gripping it tightly and taking great comfort in the solid warmth she found there. When she opened her eyes to discover him watching her with concern and love in his beautiful eyes, it helped center her enough to say, "We'll figure it out. We'll look into financial aid programs, personal loans—whatever we need to do to get you the money. You're going to be a doctor like you've always dreamed, Colleen. I promise."

And she meant it. Colleen's future wasn't ruined. Not if she had anything to say about it.

"I miss you, Shannon. Maybe I should just forget about being a doctor and move out to Fortune, too."

And give up on her childhood dream? Umm, no. "Med school first, Leenie. You're going to make it through."

Big, shaky sigh. "Okay, fine."

"I'll call you later and we'll get it sorted out."

"Thanks, sis."

"It's what I'm here for," Shannon said, grinning fondly. "Love you, talk soon."

And the only thing she could think as she hung up on her sister to continue watching the news report was that she was really glad she'd had the nerve to make her own choices. That she'd chosen her own life, even when it hadn't been easy. For the rest of her life she was going to be proud of herself for finding her path. One that included opening up her riding school on Pine Creek Ranch and spending every night snuggled into the arms of the man she loved. The man who loved and accepted her unequivocally—regardless of her issues and struggles.

It was a blessing.

She watched the news play out on screen, and it hit her how calm she felt about it, about watching her father's karma come back to him. Why was she so unemotional about it?

Because they were his choices, his mistakes. He'd made his world what it was.

Life was about choices.

And she'd made the choice to find the courage to face her fears. Because of it she was finally free. Free from the past, and free to build the future she'd always dreamed. Most importantly, she was free to just be herself, imperfect as she was, knowing she was fully, truly loved.

"Hey, Sean?" she said.

"Yes, *a mhuirnin*?" he replied, bringing their joined hands to his lips and kissing her knuckles tenderly.

A big, huge smile spread slowly across her face. "I'm really glad I chose you."

And that statement couldn't have been truer.

Jennifer Seasons's steamy new series continues!

Keep reading for a sneak peek at
the next book in her
Fortune, Colorado series:

TALKING DIRTY

Coming July 2015 from Avon Impulse.

TALKING DIRTY

An Excerpt From

TALKING DIRTY

Jake Stone has always been an outsider, even in his home-town. So when the town's shy librarian, Apple Woodman, comes trying to sniff out his family history for a book she's writing, he decides he's had enough. He'll give her the answers she seeks—at a price: one piece of clothing for every question she wants to ask. Apple's willing to play his game. After all, it's only clothes... It's not like they're really baring their hearts—right?

APPLE SHIFTED AND walked into the pub, her vintage sundress swishing around her knees flirtatiously. Barely noticing the brewpub's patrons or the live band that was playing on the patio, she went straight to the bar without waiting for Jake. She wanted a few seconds to plot and get it straight in her head before blurting out her new proposition.

She was pretty darn sure she was on to something.

Jake joined her at the bar and she took a deep, steadying breath. And then she placed her elbows onto the bar, leaned forward, and let her cleavage do the talking.

He scowled.

Of course he did. He was always scowling around her. Earlier had merely been his five-minute reprieve. "Put those away before you hurt someone."

Now he was sounding downright grumpy too. Huh. Funny thing. "Why would I do that?" she asked and gave her girls a little squeeze with her elbows. He muttered under his breath and scowled some more. Good. "I don't see anyone here complaining."

Not that anyone could, really. Her back was to the tables. Jake was the only one who got the full display, exactly as she'd intended.

"I'm complaining." He practically growled and yanked a white bar towel off its holder and began polishing the bar top.

He sounded surly, but Apple knew a secret about Jake, one that she was not at all ashamed to take advantage of now. "Why? Because you've been trying to scam a peek at my boobs since I started growing them in sixth grade and haven't been successful?" She tipped her head to the side and blinked all big and innocent behind her oversized reading glasses. "Are you jealous?"

He scoffed at that—*after* he glanced at her chest. She *totally* had him. "Of what? All the cases of blue balls your rack gave me when I was fifteen?"

More or less, yes.

"What if I offered to make up for all those missed opportunities? All those Spin the Bottles and Sixty Seconds in Heaven that didn't pan out?"

Jake stopped wiping the bar and pegged her with a look, his dark eyes filled with barely reined-in skepticism. "And how would you do that, juicy fruit?" he asked, referencing her childhood nickname—the one *he'd* given her the year she came into her body.

When they were teenagers, he'd been borderline obsessed with her body. And she couldn't blame him. He wasn't the only one. When all the other girls in school had barely been filling A-cups, she'd been rocking her current double Ds by the time she was fifteen. It still made her laugh good-naturedly at all the ways Jake and some of the other boys used to try to "accidentally" catch her topless. Not all at the same time, mind you. Individually, and at different times throughout her youth. Her over-developed-for-her-age body had been the subject of a lot of attention back then, that was for sure.

Thank God some things *do* change.

And if letting Jake finally see her topless was going to get him to actually open up and tell her what she needed to know about that first settlement in Fortune, then by all means she'd take her shirt off. It was worth it to her.

More to the point, she was that desperate.

Being a published author had always been her dream. And she was *this close*. She'd be an idiot *not* to flash him her goods. Only this time he wasn't offering to pay her his hard-earned summer lawn-mowing job money—and she was no longer such an innocent little good girl. Besides, it was just Jake. They'd known each other since she was three.

Her mind did a sudden flashback to the summer before Jake turned seventeen, instantly taking her back to that heat-drenched August when she was a curious and shy fifteen, and how his hungry gaze had followed her everywhere,

Apple took a deep breath. "I'm offering a trade. If you finally speak to me, I'll show you my breasts like you've wanted me to for years."

Jake laughed at that. "What makes you think I'm still interested?"

Apple gave him a level look, unfazed. "Because you're a guy."

He merely shrugged, his broad, defined shoulders moving under his faded green T-shirt. Then he slid her a cunning glance from the corner of his eye. "Maybe I am. But you're going to have to do better than that weak attempt if you want me talking, sweet thing."

Suddenly unsure, Apple replied cautiously, because one just never knew with Jake. "What else do you want?" And then she thought of everything she'd tried already and it had her exasperated all over again, so she added on a frustrated rush, "What's it going to take to get you to finally spill your family's story?"

The look he shot her had her slowly straightening from the bar, her pulse skittering. She'd never seen that particular gleam in his eye before. It was dark and intense and unreadable. Dangerous even.

She swallowed hard.

Then he placed his elbows on the bar and imitated her by leaning forward across the bar toward her. He didn't stop until they were almost nose-to-nose and she could see amber flecks in his chocolate eyes. "Here's the deal, all right? If you really want me to talk about my myself, my family—hell, about *all* my frigging secrets because I know you and you're too damned nosy and won't stop with just my ancestors—" He stopped suddenly and took a deep breath, his last words hanging suspended between them. But his gaze held steady on her as one uncomfortable heartbeat, then two, passed before he continued speaking more animatedly, seeming to be building up steam about something, "Shit, you won't stop until you've taken up permanent residence inside my head and know things about me I don't even care to understand. Why? Because you're Apple Woodman and you can't help yourself. It's what you've always done. And you think caving in and fulfilling some outdated G-rated teenage fantasy is going to be all it'll take to get me singing about stuff I've never told *anybody*?"

He straightened from the bar and crossed his arms, his face set in stern lines as he shook his head once—just once, with impact. "Nope. No good. There's only one thing you can do." He raised a hand, his long, thick index finger pointed straight in the air.

Apple eyed him warily now as she slowly inched from the bar, feminine fear skittering across her skin. Maybe this wasn't her brightest idea, after all. "Oh yeah, what could that be?"

Jake leaned over the bar toward her again and crooked his index finger at her, urging her closer. His gaze held on hers rock steady as he smiled, slow and devastating, and said the words that sent her reeling. "If you want me to talk, juicy fruit, I get to see *all* of you naked."

About the Author

JENNIFER SEASONS has been a lifelong writer and reader. She lives with her husband and four children in the mountains of rural New England. An enormous yet lovable dog and the world's coolest cat keep them company. When she's not writing, she loves spending time with her family outdoors exploring her beautiful new home state, learning the joys of organic gardening—and if she's lucky, relaxing in her hammock under the trees with a really good book. You can find her online at www.facebook.com/jennifer.seasons.3.

Discover great authors, exclusive offers, and more at hc.com.